PRAISE FOR
COURTING the WILD TWIN

'Terrifically strange and thrilling. One for all you storytellers.'
— MELISSA HARRISON, author of
All Among the Barley

'This magical book underlines the ability of storytelling to rewrite reality while functioning as a practical — and highly personal — guide to the rewilding of the self.'
— DAVID KEENAN, author of *For the Good Times*

'*Courting the Wild Twin* revels in the fabulous — the alchemy of story, primaeval nouse and narrative. Shaw is proof of William Blake's adage that "Truth can never be told so as to be understood and not believed." A thrilling exploration of ancient ambiguity, this book digs deep into the miraculous mulch of myth.'
— DAN RICHARDS, author of *Outpost*

'A book that comprehends the forests of the soul, written with fierce courage and audacious wildness.'
— JAY GRIFFITHS, author of *Wild*

'This remarkable, powerful, provocative and timely book is about the same size as your smartphone. Carry it in your other pocket, and every time you reach for your phone, take this out instead. Give your imagination, your activism, your poetic/mythic self some soul food. That's what I did, and it delighted me every time.'

— ROB HOPKINS, author of *From What Is to What If*

'Martin Shaw turns words into stories and stories into unpredictable excursions in search of the Wild Twin within each and all. He reveals the importance of this often exiled, yet deeply necessary inner otherness, the very part that holds the secret sense of rapport and essential relatedness that entwines human nature with the heart of Mother Nature.'

— MICHAEL MEADE, author of *Awakening the Soul*

'*Courting the Wild Twin* beckons us to step through the doorway that stories create, and reveals a pathway to awakening our relationship with the world around — and with ourselves.'

— DEE DEE CHAINEY,
author of *A Treasury of British Folklore*

COURTING
the
WILD TWIN

Also by Martin Shaw

Smoke Hole (Chelsea Green Publishing, 2021)

Cinderbiter with Tony Hoagland (Graywolf Press, 2020)

The Night Wages (Cista Mystica Press, 2019)

Wolf Milk (Cista Mystica Press, 2019)

Courting the Dawn: Poems of Lorca with Stephan Harding
(Cista Mystica Press, 2019)

The Five Fathoms (Hedgespoken Press, 2018)

Mythteller Trilogy (Cista Mystica Press):

Scatterlings: Getting Claimed in the Age of Amnesia (2016)

*Snowy Tower: Parzival and the
Wet Black Branch of Language* (2014)

*A Branch from the Lightning Tree:
Ecstatic Myth and the Grace in Wildness* (2011)

COURTING
the
WILD TWIN

MARTIN
SHAW

Chelsea Green Publishing
London, UK
White River Junction, Vermont, USA

Project Manager: Sarah Kovach
Project Editor: Jonathan Rae
Copy Editor: Laura Jorstad
Proofreader: Laura Booth
Designer: Melissa Jacobson

Printed in the United States of America.
First printing February 2020.
10 9 8 7 6 5 4   23 24 25 26 27

Library of Congress Cataloging-in-Publication Data
Names: Shaw, Martin, author.
Title: Courting the wild twin / Martin Shaw.
Description: White River Junction, Vermont : Chelsea Green Publishing, [2020] |
    Series: Wild ideas series | Includes bibliographical references.
Identifiers: LCCN 2019049646 | ISBN 9781603589505 (hardcover) |
    ISBN 9781603589512 (ebook) | ISBN 9781603589529 (audiobook)
Subjects: LCSH: Twins — Mythology. | Twins — Folklore. | Myth — Psychology.
Classification: LCC BL325.T8 S53 2020 | DDC 202/.2 — dc23
LC record available at https://lccn.loc.gov/2019049646

Chelsea Green Publishing
London, UK
White River Junction, Vermont, USA
www.chelseagreen.com

For Torin Passmore,
You Little Merlin

My gratitude to Robert Bly and Gioia Timpanelli,
brilliant teachers of these intricate stories.

CONTENTS

THE CONDITION
OF WONDERING

Someone Wants to Talk to You

The business of stories is not enchantment.
The business of stories is not escape.
The business of stories is waking up.

Imagine, if you will, looking up into the dark and naming a star. You could be crouching in the moonlight outside a Dordogne cave, or peering up from a balcony in west London in the middle of a party as the music pumps, pumps, pumps. But for some reason we commit to gazing. And something happens when we, maybe rashly, give ourselves utterly to the turbulent luminosity of the universe. We start to gabble in love speech.

So there you are, looking at the star.

You could call it something like:

Flint of Whale Bone
Dream Coin of the Moon
Pale Rivet of the Sun's Own Spear
White Bridle of the Black Riders

This condition of wondering is still absolutely intact in us. It is. Amongst the loaded shopping trolleys of Walmart and Tesco, the fluorescent tech hubs, flicker-screens and finger-beckoning apps, it's still there. This raw, imaginative, holy thing.

3

There's an audacity to it, but it's what we've always done. We did it on the plains of South Dakota, we did it in the muddied byres of Shropshire, we did it on the vampiric tips of snowy Carpathian Mountains. And here's the thing: we did it to claim not ownership but connection. There's a swoon in this, a bearing witness, a startled affection growing to an awe. There is no flag planting, no home improvement planned, just giddy, magical naming. And maybe the star just named itself and used us to do it. Maybe it spoke through us for a moment. There's a health to this.

Much has been written about the human impulse to daub its spray on every living thing, to bellow the decree of its franchise, but what happens when the earth itself gives a little pushback? When it's not us lacing a brocade of dominion-speak into a voidal dark, but that actually the words themselves may be the return journey of longing from the thing itself. That there's a scrummage of inspiration that is not only human. This is a reality that has been articulated from Amazonia to Renaissance Italy, from the Yakut to the Aborigine. That words can have fur and light in them. Words can constrict, words can liberate.

Bad storytellers make spells.

Great storytellers break them.

This, now, is mostly an era of spell-making. Of tacit enchantment, of stultified imaginations and loins inflamed by so much factory-fodder lust, our relationships malfunction in their millions. We are on the island of the Lotus Eaters, curled up in the warm sleepy breeze of a Russian fairy tale as the robber steals away the Firebird. How do we wake up?

I will give you a little plot-spoiler right here. Sounds so very deceptively simple. The secret is relatedness.

Relatedness. Relatedness breeds love, and love can excavate conscience. Conscience changes the way we behave. Relatedness is how we wake up. But I am going to take a long and sometimes diffuse route to say it in the fashion that such a notion deserves. As I will repeat before the end of this book, be sceptical of the quick route. It's truly what's got us into a thousand unruly messes. And not the kind the poets praise.

There are stories about living without relatedness. They don't tend to end well. Without relatedness we dwell in a place the Inuit call the Moon Palace. The Moon Palace is a place that appears perfectly safe: we have a great view of the earth and its goings-on, but we touch nothing. We can spend years and years up there. Heartbreak will get us there. The cool of the Moon Palace is a very dangerous place to be. Likely there comes a point where you want to come back down. The old ones say the earth is only three steps down from the Moon Palace, but we have to keep our eyes open as we descend. If we are unconscious we become spiders that cause webs to trap everyone around us. In other words, we cast spells.

The three steps down from the Moon Palace are instigated by longing to connect, for heat, opinion, passion, the dusty market square of life. Relatedness is the way back, but doing it with awareness.

So. I want to know if the earth will still reveal its secret names to us. The only way we can know is if we as a culture take those three steps.

This is a book that makes a case for a world that still seeks our eyes on it. Our admiration. Our care. Our artfulness. And from that comes a particular kind of hope.

Amongst the clear-eyed of us, *hope* is becoming a word laced with some doubt, and rightly so. At least from a certain point of departure. When I speak to the climatic conditions of our time through the voice of a pundit, philosopher, attender to the seemingly divinatory crackle of 'the facts of the matter', I feel a blue note of utter sorrow that I can't come back from. But I do not choose to look at the conditions of our times only through those prisms; there is another, more ancient device. Story.

Of course, myths speak of the endings of things, of any number of ruptures and rebirths, and are often thoroughly drubbed with grief and the tragic. Ragnarok or Revelation is always at hand. Some beast is always slouching towards Bethlehem. Everything falls apart. The child crawls into the snow and is not seen. But over time a shoot will emerge from a heap of ashes. A girl will walk back from the forest speaking a language no one has ever heard. This is less optimism, more observation.

I should reveal my hand here.

I don't believe our prayers always land this side of the river. I believe in a receiver. Even though what may wind its way back to us is in some costume we never expected. Stories can actually be a kind of praying, a back-and-forth between us and the earth and its myriad dimensions. This is absolutely not the same thing as a wish list to the heavenly.

If you think you've only got yourself for company, you are on the quick road to crazy.

I'm not telling you what to pray to, the celestial-or-otherwise shape of the thing, but find something to adore and keep talking to it. It'll regulate anxiety at the very least. It won't remove grief, not useful remorse, but the grind of chronic or acute fear can find its expression as an alchemical progression, not a final destination.

Stories worth their salt don't tell us to get cranked up with either naive hope or vinegar-tinged despair. Stories tell us to keep attending to the grace. Keep an eye on the miraculous. It is not for us to blow the candle out; only the gods can do that. You simply don't do that as a storyteller. You have corrupted yourself at that point, broken covenant with magical possibility. You have forgotten your tribal function, your metaphysical directive.

So for a moment, I ask us to entertain possibilities, that's all. Put down the podcast or latest gut-churning piece of will-draining bad news, and let's crouch by the fire in the old way that is forever new. Somebody wants to talk to you.

So, the old ones say, the old ones say, the old ones say:

To cast the language of relatedness, you have to know you have a wild twin.

The earth has scattered many clues around you so you pick their scent up.

But who are the old ones?

They are your invested dead, the ones who wrap foxglove round the pale horns of cattle and push back the very gates of dawn just so your dreams can claim contact a little longer. The old ones inhabit the nattering jawbone and mottled tongue of someone who suddenly speaks words you desperately need to hear. They make their lives by hand, wear their wealth on their body, mutter to you in underground ways that make you writhe with both pleasure and appropriate distress when you really detect the mandate. An old one is the night sigh of chalk-white cliffs when all the twinkly villages of Sussex have settled into their bedded nests and children sleep happily, dreaming only of cake. They are the whole bright universe talking to you. Of course they know about the wild twin. They are its grandparents.

Who is the wild twin?

I first caught the perfume of my wild twin by walking with muddy boots through wet grasses to my scrubby woodland den as a six-year-old. As the trees swirled I caught a scent and started to cry without understanding. I wove a pheasant feather in my hair. I hear it now in the owl court who hoot across the frost grass and moon-touched lawns of my cottage. There's more than book smarts in that chill delirium. These are not domestic tones, not corralled sounds, but loose as Dartmoor ponies on the hill. They give me ecstasy. Not safety, not contentment, certainly not ease, not peace, but ecstasy. It's almost painful. Makes me restless.

I also felt the wild twin when I lost the girl I loved the most. I felt it when attending the sickness of another. I felt it when exhausted, heart-sore, bewildered and despairing. I felt it when I attended to the sorrows of life in all their radical, unruly agency.

The wild twin is not unique to me; you have one, everyone has one. That's the message from the old stories. That the day you were born, a twin was thrown out the window, sent into exile. That it wanders the woods and the prairies and the cities, lonely in its whole body for you. It rooms in abandoned houses in South Chicago. Someone saw her once on a Dorset beach in winter. They are always asking after you.

It lives in the feeling when the ruddy mud of the Nile squeezes between your toes, when moonlight slips from the mouth of a heron, when you play cards with a delightful villain. It's going to push you towards ruin on occasion, and has a lot of generosity towards kids. It will hide your laptop and send a thousand wild geese processing over your tent on an October dusk. The wild twin is the vintner of the blood-wine of your many private battles, and sells it in highly prized bottles to remote Armenian queens.

It is incorrigible, melodramatic, and has only your best interests at heart.

Know your twin and you will become distracted by fiery angels languishing round the water cooler, you will beat your palms to drums no one else can hear and subtle ideas will fly from you. At least that's what I hear. The wild twin doesn't fetishise surety, embezzle guarantees or even really believe they exist. It hides chocolate in the pockets of your scruffy-haired nephews and whispers forgiveness as it walks through the gardens we have neglected to tend. It hands us a spade.

I believe that in the labour of becoming a human, you have to earnestly search this character out, as it has something crucial for you with it. It has your life's purpose tucked up in its pocket. If there was something you were here to do in these few, brief years, you can be sure that the wild twin is holding the key.

Wildness attracts everybody but appears to be in short supply. Not feral, not hooligan, not brawling, but the regal wild. The sophisticated wild. So you should be gathering by now that this book is about locating your long-abandoned twin and courting it home. We're going to use two old fairy tales to do it. And note the word *court*. This is a protracted affair, this locating, with the possibility of many missteps, bruised shins and hissed exchanges. Though they long for you, the twin may not broker relationship easily if you've been separated for many years; she wants to know you're serious. We'll cover the complexity of such a reunion as we go. They want to give you a bang on the ear and a kiss on the lips all at the same time.

Lorca claims that the goblin of trouble, *duende,* is this thing that evokes such a twin. Duende is knowledge that this all ends, that our wings have rusty blades attached that scrape the dusty limits of the dirt. I wrote a moment ago that the perfume of the wild twin provided me not with a sense of safety but with one of restlessness. The world pushes you into poetry by withdrawing something, not giving it. The greatest poems are not written by the woman who got that last kiss; they are written by the woman who didn't. And in that absence, that heart-sore knowledge, dwells the duende. The grit, the limp, the slap, the push-back. We begin to understand why polite society has exiled the wild twin.

But the cost of its absence is so terribly high. We exist in its consequence.

No twin, and we, as Robert Bly used to say, preserve life but don't give life. There's not the holy rashness that invokes the spiritual energies of the universe. The wild twin rolls the dice a little. Without eros, without risk, there's no culture worth making. So this is a dangerous business, calling out to these brooding, exiled energies. But truth be told and nailed to the tavern wall, it's far, far more dangerous not to.

I'm not sure we ever really, properly, catch up with our wild twin, buy matching sweaters. The pursuit is the thing, the glimpse is the thing, the jolt of their quixotic nature may be barometer enough for one lifetime. But never to search? Well, that's missing out on life altogether.

Amazingly, even the story of the Wild Twin has a twin. And we'll work into that story in the later stages of this book.

But let's begin our first tale. We explore it in several sections. If you would like to encounter it whole first of all, then please go to the end of the book and then let's meet back here.

COURTING
THE WILD TWIN

THE LINDWORM

*O*H *THERE WAS A KINGDOM*
of curlews and inkberry, snowy mountain
and tangled byre, a kingdom of bristling meadows and secretive pools of water only you know
about. The hawk circled such pools, and fish
darted swiftly under the surface.

In the centre of the kingdom presided a king
and queen. Gracious and attentive to their people, distributors of favours, settlers of disputes,
throwers of banquets, you never heard a bad
word about them. But at night a sorrowful grief
hung between them. They could not conceive a
child. This nibbled away at the queen, slowed
her every step, and so she took herself off to the
surrounding forest, hoping a stroll would calm
her anguish.

Under the bough of an oak tree she met
an old woman, who recognised the tension

in the young woman's face. When the queen
unburdened herself of her concern, the crone
claimed she had a remedy for the issue, and if
she followed her instructions exactly, then all
would be well. She spoke:

"You need to give voice to what you truly
desire. Get your breath on it. Tonight at dusk,
walk to the north-west part of the garden
and, as you go, speak everything you wish to
see arise. Finally, speak the last words into a
double-handled cup, flip the cup onto the dark
soil and go to bed. In the morning there will be
two flowers under the cup. One red, one white.
Eat the white, but under no circumstances the
red. Eat the white and you will have that which
you cherish the most."

At the end of the day, the queen did just that.
She strolled and spoke, whispered and crooned
everything that was in her heart. Gave every
fissure of longing voice, then blew into the cup
and flipped it onto the soil. That night she made
love with her husband.

In the morning she walked to the cup and
turned it over. Just as the old woman had said:
the red and white flower. She remembered
exactly the instructions of the crone.

Ah, why do we do this?

Why do we do this?

Why do we do this?

Before she knew it she was on all fours
gobbling up the red flower, every last bit of it. In
the doing of it, her body rang out like a struck
bell of rapture. Every nerve ending accomplished
itself in an exfoliation of ecstasy.

And then, slowly, she came back to herself.
This wasn't what the old woman suggested. In fact
it was the opposite of what she suggested. Guiltily
she reached for the white flower and consumed
it. She and her husband made a decision – no
one needed to know – it was settled.

Well, the old woman's magics worked; she
immediately felt new life nibbling at her energy
and nine months later she went into labour. A
centre that had been barren was about to demonstrate its fertility again.

The strangest thing happened: it was not
a child that exclaimed itself from the queen's
womb but a small black snake, a worm. Such was
the shock of the moment, the midwife grabbed
the writhing serpent and hurled it far out of the
window into the darkness of the forest. Only
minutes later a baby boy was born, and the snake
was forgotten, never to be spoken of.

Years passed and the boy became a young
man. A man that wished for a wife, a love, a
companion. And that sort of thing requires

searching for; it requires a quest. He went to his parents, and they gave him permission to travel out and see if such a one existed. They gifted him a white horse and white saddle and bridle for the occasion.

Such high spirits as he galloped from the castle, heart a-rat-a-tat-tat in his chest.

Farther he went into the forest, past the typical hunting spots he had enjoyed, far deep into the dreaming. He came to a crossroads, and it was there that his life utterly changed.

Rearing up before him was a huge, scaled, black serpent. Steam from its nostrils and a raw bellow from its snapping jaw: "Older brothers marry first! Older brothers marry first!"

Sensibly, the young man fled, but for the rest of the day every crossroads he came to there was a serpent bellowing: "Older brothers marry first!"

Exhausted, shaken, he returned to his parents that night with a question:

"Is there anything about my birth that may have slipped your mind to tell me? Anything involving a furious black snake that claims to be my older brother?"

His parents went blank at the query. We don't know if they recalled or not. Whether they were stalling or innocent of memory. What we do know is that all three of them visited the midwife and asked her the same question. By now such a tiny woman she could have taken residence in a matchbox, she finally spoke: "No, no, no, no, no, no, yes, no, no, no, no." They heard that *yes* secreted amongst the *no*s, and suddenly she was adrift in confession.

"Well. I don't quite like to recall, but yes, maybe definitely there was a wee black worm that shot from the queen. A terrible-looking thing. I held it for a fraction of a second then hurled it into the dark and the rain. And now look at you, handsome prince, why bother thinking of a little freak like that when we can enjoy you?"

The family went very quiet. But it was a useful kind of a quiet, a deepening, and from that deepening something extraordinary was hatched. The king spoke:

"If it is true that this is your brother, then we must not send hunters into the forest to slaughter it. We must send the poets, the musicians, the storytellers to court it from its lair. It needs to be with us. It needs to come home. We need to make a home for the serpent."

And that was exactly what happened. In the belly of the castle, a room was filled with hay to make a vast nest, and slowly, through kind words and lively music, the black snake

19

slouched towards its family. It was so vast the doors had to be widened to get him in; tapestries got scorched by his breath. But by the end of the month, it had happened: the snake was in residence.

And from the centre of the castle, all heard the bellow:

"Older brothers marry first!"

Nothing Grows

It is the way of fairy tales to be alerted to a problem early. The generative centre of things, the king and queen, cannot conceive a child. Quite what provoked the lack of fertility is not clear, only that it squats emphatically behind all the good deeds the sovereigns provide. They are not villains or hypnotised by greed, they are not toxic, and yet, still, things have ground to a halt.

Life preserving but not life giving: remember that thought of Bly. That's what the wagons are circled around here. Nothing is harmed, but nothing thrives either. This is a less overt malaise than tyrant and tanks, but it's a malaise nonetheless.

If you've ever laboured to be a 'nice guy' over your own moral instincts, a 'good girl' and not shake the status quo, then you'll know things can get pretty arid. Dried up.

There's more than a hint of that here. There can be shiny teeth and perfect popularity but the three strange angels no longer knock at your door, the sirens no longer wreck your ships as they are perfectly entitled to do. We all need a few sunken ships.

Being in charge can get awfully stale.

So we are not in the presence of tyrants, but a subtler stagnation. Too much civic duty can lack the sheer, thrusting eros required for new life to burst forth. For that we have to go to the liminal forest. We have to enter the wayward.

Entering the Wayward

It could be desert, tundra, a lonely road on the way home from the fair, but the change of gear required always happens some distance from the centre of power. A shakedown is required, and a different kind of threshold to experience. So two things occur in the story in this moment:

1. We go from the curation of the human to the wild. The Castle to the Forest.

2. We receive information from an older person. There is a move between generations.

We are out of straight lines and sculpted hedges and into knobbly tree roots, elk scat, the scrape of a mystic's fiddle. Sideways things, crooked genius over straightforward intelligence. Our thoughts bang into things out there, become more porous, expansive, nutty, dreamlike. To be sure, there are gradients of this in our modern lives: from daydreaming on a train to fasting on a mountain, but one way or another we shape-leapt a little.

And what we meet out there is older than us. In a culture of worth this means they know more, are closer to God, have made a covenant with the unexpected. Where is your liminal forest? What shady place is allotted in your life to let your thinking lope and purr and get old-womanly?

There are books that may bend us sufficiently to expand this way, as well as people and animals.

What area of your home contorts your imagination? Where are you smartest? Most eccentric? What time of day provokes the liminal?

I have a variety of desks at my cottage, and I notice I write quite differently on all of them. And day and night intelligence are quite different too. Translating Lorca these last five years is a masterclass in the night. Novalis heads in this direction, Hölderlin and Blake too. It's astonishing how many teachers are wandering around the quadrants of our imagination, coughing quietly and gesturing that we may want to sign up to their class. It's an unnecessary misery to feel that the honeycomb of previous centuries is not available. It is. We just have to convince the Grand Old Ones that we're serious. Seriousness is indicated by fidelity. To keep showing up.

I have a very literal relationship to forests too. After almost twenty years as a wilderness rites of passage guide, I have seen what time alone in such a place does to a human (even the so-called modern variety). They all meet the Old Woman in some fashion, though it may take some years to tease out her riddles.

I would imagine many of you know what a wilderness vigil or vision quest entails, so I won't overlabour it. Four days fasting and sitting in a wild place. But it's worth flagging up its three stages: severance, threshold, return. To leave the human community, encounter the wild and return. This almost comically simple dynamic underpins an enormous amount of both ritual practices and mythologies from all over the world. We can amplify it clearly in the story of *The Lindworm* and many more. Why do we witness it again and again and again? Because it fits the human experience of living, it's not an abstraction, it is a triadic leathering that we all sigh and grunt with acknowledgement over when its tapestry is displayed in art, story, theatre. We know it.

The castle can be a place of spirit, but the forest offers soul. There are levels of sophistication to this description but I need to exaggerate to make the picture more distinct. Spirit lifts, soul deepens. Spirit is a spark; soul is a drop of water. Spirit is a great idea; soul is deep knowing. We absolutely need both.

Liminal information is often irrational, hard to decipher, imagistic not conceptual. It's often unsettling because it rarely conforms to the norm. It never smooths anything over. There are few liminal coffee mornings, though brainstorming or mind-mapping sessions are an attempt to kick-start the process. It distils slowly, is reluctant to rush, is furry not smooth, may even carry the perspective of curly bellied baby mice and gossiping panthers.

That's the point of the old vigils: to be broken open and shaken up by the great forces of the universe. The spirits are canyon-deep and as varied as snowflakes. And let's not shy away from this truth: there's a slaughter out there – something has to be traded for this bounty. It's usually the child that you were. In a tribe dependent on ingenuity and resilience, they need to know you've grown properly, otherwise you are too much weight to carry. It seems imperative that in this human-growing process you get in touch with more than just people round a fire chewing it all over. You need rook squawks, spirit winds, sparks of magic and the croak of the ancestral dead in the mix. These things are simply more tangible in the wild. They step forward.

Night Falls on Her Wishes

Sometimes in other stories, old women of the forest counsel silence in the completion of a spiritual task, to build interior energies, but it's the opposite here. The queen needs to make some space for her own desires. She needs to chew on them, formulate them, sing them, brood on them so golden eggs of possibility crack open on her tongue.

Speaking like this is a form of thought: oral thought. Things happen when you start to speak. Things get chivvied along. Thoughts leap and contort. Note the old woman said nothing about having to speak to other humans, but to take her longing to the dusk, the air, the soil, the garden. The advice to the queen is to spread out amongst the universe, not get red-taped into the drudgery and gossip of the court.

Thinking in myth grows us in how to talk. Not in thesaurus-speak but in image power. So we find out what we think by risking words. The words themselves are animate, revealing secret meetings within the soul that the mind hadn't quite caught up with yet. I always see the queen gabbling and muttering as she walks the garden, surprising herself, rather than launching into a readily prepared speech. It risks spontaneity.

The breathing into the cup and the flip is interesting. After the wider, spoken stroll, suddenly we are into an enclosed space, a boundaried, curvaceous world to carry the wish down into the soil. There is a sense of distillation, of narrowing, of a deepening to this wider rumination. By the time she flips the cup, she's got specific. And those two handles seem like ears, listening out to the response of the earth. Night falls on her wishes.

There is a great intelligence at work in this section of the tale. Fairy tales understand the immediate impulse when we hear: "Don't open that door, don't gobble that flower." For every intention we have, there is an equally strong counter-intention, and sometimes that hidden intention creates a more unruly but ultimately more rewarding narrative in our lives. A transgression occurs that has a whiff of efficacy to it.

This is a canny understanding of how we operate below the waves, and shows us that the crone has something of the trickster to her, some sass, plenty of wit. We know as the queen gobbles the red flower we are witnessing desire in extremis, the very thing the old woman encouraged. This is not 'good girl' behaviour, this is not decision by committee, this has not been road-tested by study groups. This is happening right now, bidden by urge.

But of course every happening has a consequence. It births something. Now she has the attention of Dionysus as well as Hera, the eruptive, regenerative force of nature as well as marriage. At the moment of consumption, she switched temples.

Even in modern life we lurch in and out of initiatory states, we just may not recognise them as such. One of the ways we recognise such a transition is pantingly close is when we start acting in new or unexpected ways. Some dozing part of our character suddenly wakes and staggers to the fore, and only change will do. I would call this switching temples.

Religious, agnostic, atheist: we all serve in some kind of temple. All serve something. So what is the libation required when you switch from white to red flower? The shopping lists and insurance policies have been replaced by devilishly erotic love poetry and a propensity for singing the sun up. Usually the temple switching is not seamless, rarely elegant. An affair may provoke it, boredom may engender it, but its passport stamp is usually rupture. The Zen temple is scattered with single-malt bottles, and a hangover settles in dank air.

Here's the rub, the subtle point. Myth tells us we live in the tension between flowers, or between castle and forest; we are not to choose one entirely over the other. We are not to fetishise the hell raisers any more than we are the choir masters. That crossroads is a complex position, the position of that much-maligned entity: an adult. The final section of the book will address this again.

So who do you serve? Are you in the correct arrangement? Is there a way we can taste the red flower without burning the whole house down? Myth suggests so, rites of passage suggest so.

A healthy psyche is alert to the reality that we aren't lived by a myth but by myths, plural. We could think of each mythic narrative having a temple attached. In the course of a day, we may serve in several of them. The diligent young parent may be apprenticing to discipline, but needs a side of time in the wild to not grow brittle. This is where Artemis rocks up. The problems arise when we suck on the mono-myth, the one temple. That's when we get a little nutty. We need a little wiggle room. I'll pick this theme up again a little down the trail.

Communicate with Beauty

My older and wisers always drilled this fact into me: *what you exile will grow hostile towards you.*

Think of the genie who, on being freed from the bottle, says: "If you'd come ten years ago I would have given you a wish, come five years ago I would have thanked you, but come now I'm going to kill you." The mood turns, doesn't it? What got hurled away so roughly has not been suckling on the milk of human kindness. It's peered many times through the tree line as the affluent brother practices his fencing to polite applause and a passing of the cucumber sandwiches.

This scene always causes some rueful reflection on what got chucked away. When I was in my twenties I exiled the one who examined the small print on a book contract, remembered the birthdays of my relatives, got back to a friend's question with any urgency. I'm ashamed of this, and am still working on it. Others I know can't financially value their work effectively, or are paralysed on a dance floor, at odds in their own body's expression. We've all got something seething out in the forest, peering in at us and spitting on the dirt. What haven't we valued?

It's possible that far from an internal reading of the story, we may have lived this out as a family dynamic – we were literally the unfavoured sibling. 'The forest' can still abide inside many modern homes. The question is, do we want to settle for that? What on earth do we do about it?

A start is to broker communication with beauty. Now, what a serpent regards as beautiful is an interesting conjecture, but it's a way to begin. There's no demands, no aggression, no cease-and-desist order, there's actually a little tenderness. The details are not plentiful at this moment, only that it's enough to get the serpent to the castle.

Although beauty has its broad strokes that most of us recognise – dusk, snowfall, the beaming face of a child – there is also something profoundly individual about what we regard as beautiful. When I was younger I grew wary of what we could think of as the glossy, pre-mediated variety. I needed something rawer, something that felt true. Something that cut much away. I needed to see the wound. Cultural and personal. I needed its articulation. I wanted to burn everything down. Blunt, powerful music served that purpose for a while.

But that pesky alchemical insistence within myth never goes away, that we acknowledge deeply the wound but can't languish there as its final articulation, its last alliteration. Beauty is created not just by desire but by diligence. By circling again and again like a hawk round the well to what truly sends you both dizzy with admiration but also utterly focused in service. Be mastered by beauty is what I'm saying. Be defeated by it. Rise to it in the weepy faithfulness of your response.

Lorca tells us in a hundred different ways that the finest flamenco is conducted by the wild old woman in black with the grievously stooped back, and her wily, gloriously rotund husband with his glitter-gold-tooth grin. They drag the time-bound into the timeless. They bring the wayward nobility of ageing *clackerty-clackerty-clack* onto the creaking wood of life's rambunctious dance floor, a hundred horse skulls sequestered underneath to improve the acoustics (*which was a real thing, by the way, in old East Anglia*).

Whatever beauty was communicated to the serpent, I think it had to have some of that grit in it.

We note that the serpent initiated this. They are not at the business end of a rabid hunt. He's named his stipulation: older brothers marry first. The serpent wants a bride. It doesn't mean he's in any way ready for one, but the heat of desire is there. Like his mother the queen, the worm is speaking his desire. He's saying what he wants. The exiled requires union, the dark requires a mate, it demands visibility. It's a demand for consciousness.

I have fun imagining a therapist standing in front of the beast and attempting to mirror back his feelings: "I can see that you're angry. I get that. It must have been a lonely time out there in the forest." I jest, but this would be a reality on many couches around the world. Therapists get singed on occasion; it's a contact sport.

The serpent carries massive energy with it, that heavy, curling tail, the belly of fire. And we need such a divine, potent resource. As we go further into the story, we can imagine quite what it's like to have a serpent as part of

30

our home, our character, our will, not just a rumour in a far-off forest. The ass-kicker has arrived.

*T*HEY MESSAGED ALL corners of the land: 'dark prince seeks bride', and the response was keen. One of the applicants was confirmed and brought to the castle. After a tour of the grounds, she was taken into a low-lit room with a priest. A vast, dark presence filled half of it. As she repeated the vows, a scaly tail wrapped itself around her legs and hips three times. In the morning there was nothing but bones in the hay, and a worm calling: "Older brothers marry first!"

You can be sure that after a few more applicants, the position took on less glamour, and rumours started to circulate. It was 'the castle you went into and never came out'. The messengers still circulated, but for a few months everything went quiet. Even the rats were leaving the cellars of the place, let alone the servants. Albatross albatross albatross. Mary Celeste.

With this in mind, it was a big surprise when a message came through from the daughter of a

31

shepherd. That she would marry the prince, but wished for a year and a day to prepare herself.

The shepherd had heard the rumours and was distraught at his daughter's decision. She herself was not quite sure why she'd made it. As always in times of unrest, she took herself to the woods to think things through, feel things through.

As she sat under the shade of an oak bough, an old woman walked clean out of the tree. Not round the tree, not towards the tree, out of the tree.

For the second time in our tale, an old woman offered instruction:

"It was a brave thing to take this on, but wiser still to give yourself time to figure out a plan.

"If I was you, if I was you, if I was you, I would sew twelve nightshirts for your wedding night.

"Embroider especially around the heart. I would insist that one bath of water and ashes was prepared, and one of milk, and two great scrubbing brushes supplied. The baths and the brushes are to be left in the bed chamber. And quite what do you do with this advice? Well, that's what the rest of your preparation time is to figure out." And with that she walked back into the core of the tree.

For the rest of her time, the young woman laboured on the shirts. She'd never worked with that kind of intricacy before, and her hands ached and fingers got pricked by the needle. But she worked on, educating herself in both delicacy and stamina, persistence and imagination. She thought about quite what it was she was marrying, and how to approach such a thing.

A Vast, Dark Presence

What is life like when you don't know what it is you're marrying? Harshly put, it implies you are naive. Gullible. Didn't read that small print. A terrible deal occurs in the fairy tale *The Handless Maiden,* when a father barters away his daughter to a demon by not realising who he's talking to when the deal is struck. In the Greek myth of Psyche and Eros, it is clear that the centre of each wedding requires a death. Psyche has black banners at her wedding to the serpent, out-of-tune fiddles and swooping vultures; the scene is clear. This needs a woman's clarity, not a girl's hopes.

We may end up as crumbling bones in the hay before we literally wise up. Any scene that repeats itself against our better judgement has a touch of this story in it. We can be gobbled up almost a dozen times before, finally, we retrace our steps a little. There has to be a different way of doing this. It appears that although it was an elegant and touching scene when the musicians and poets brought back the serpent into the castle, much deeper work was still to be done. And for a while it remains ugly. We are seeing that simple trust is not enough to negotiate with darkness. Fingers crossed and a big smile will get us incinerated.

The detail that the servants are leaving the castle is interesting. People are losing faith, or even running scared. A community notices that sort of thing. Folks talk, and the giddy sheen of marrying a prince has long, long left the invitation. It's no longer a magnetic proposal; the rumour is that it's grievously dangerous. And into the danger comes the daughter of a shepherd.

A shepherd's daughter, though we may romanticise the thought, is not usually in the running for marrying a prince. Complex strata of class stand between that possibility. Maybe if she'd applied at the beginning, she would have had no hearing. But now this marginal, unusual figure is given an audience, and even has the smarts to negotiate a year and a day to prepare. That's extraordinary, shows leadership.

Leadership and chutzpah. The girl's got front. The story tells us there's a tree in the forest she likes to sit by. A place she can deepen. There is already some move towards interiority. The story wants us to presume that this is the same crone that spoke earlier to the queen; she is a baseline energy that emerges now and then to keep the story rolling. She is a still small voice that can be trusted.

When an ancient energy wakes up in you, it's likely to rattle your cage with image not concept; that's how it's always been done. Images seem to be how the soul carriages its messages to you. To move and confound you, to unsettle, to get you to work. These lively impulses are going to broker instructions that are to be carried out, and it's only in the carrying out that you will come to find quite why you were doing it in the first place. I know that takes some pondering as an idea, but I hope you'll entertain it. Walking blind a little. Falling into the nettles.

She doesn't wink at the young girl and slip her an ABC-type map for the journey. She just gives the instruction. Up ahead are countless hours of frustration as we learn to construct wedding shirts, pricked fingers, patience and that attention to the heart.

I first started to work on the wedding shirts in my twenties. It looked to the outside world like a scruffy kid buying Pablo Neruda's *The Captain's Verses* and scuttling off to my tent to learn by heart one of the poems. I loved Neruda's understanding of the dark side in those poems to his wife, how he wore his shadow like a cloak. Jealousy, aggression, domination, all of these unmentionable capacities were writ large in the book. They sung their true sound and his angels scuffed their boots in the eager pollen of my mind. The book had many other tones, but he let the rough squalls and scudding clouds of grief into his praise words.

He let it all hang out. He wasn't embarrassed. This wasn't persona. He didn't edit his weather patterns.

This was the beginning of education, what the troubadours would think of as an educated heart. Whenever sewing is featured in a fairy tale, it implies that the one who sews is weaving their life to the Otherworld. The needle draws in close an intelligence secreted in the Milky Way, and then draws out the deep keening of our own heart for understanding, knowledge, maybe, one day, wisdom.

It could be that every shirt she sewed mourned the death of an earlier bride. Maybe she pricked one drop of blood into the deep red patterning around the heart. This shirt-making is about not getting incinerated, not fetishising ashes as the only way to depth. It's not. We don't need to set fire to our lives or marry a psychopath to deepen. I mean, it happens, but it's not a recommendation.

It's back to a word I've written about many times. *Tempering.* You get complicit with the whorls in the wood you lathe and the many temperaments of love's engine, rather than joyriding the thing and crashing into a wall over and over again. That provides a lot of drama but little nourishment for those around you. It doesn't give life, rather ends it.

I try to limit my public forays into etymology, others do it far better, but connections to tempering are: *temper* – from the Old English *temprian,* meaning 'to moderate excess, to regulate'. The Latin *tempus* has a possible route of 'stretch', and an example often given is of tuning an instrument, to make it taut.

Every time I have wrestled either an angel or a devil, I have been usefully but catastrophically defeated. But I have always had the distinct impression of being tuned, of something being burnt off, of giving libation to the god of limits. I see *tempering* as a more useful word than *initiation* in many cases. It brings up fewer associations with particular age ranges and a more circular, more regular encounter. And one that makes us hum like the taut string on a lyre. Tempering, if we are really paying attention, will be a constant our whole life.

We live in a speedy world, with a kind of faux-Hermes urgency to communication. *Just do it.* To hang back like the shepherd's daughter does, to learn a skill, to befriend solitude (remember, the old woman leaves again), shows her capacity to do something very rare – to delay gratification. Culture is defined not by what you gained but by what you were prepared to live without. This emphasis on sacrifice is not sadism; it's one of life's essential currencies.

When is enough, *enough?*

This is not a marriage with dizziness at its core, or wistfulness, but preparation. Sobriety. As we know, a story like this touches us on many levels. It can be experienced as how a society sifts its aggressions and malice to the surface, how you negotiate the turbulence of love to another, how you get conscious about your own hurts and resentments and all the exiled energy tangled up in them. And that's just from the human, immediate perspective. I would always caution against too literal a reading of the story, however. That's a way to experience the ornamentation of the narrative but not its depths. That way the less agreeable elements stay at a distance. That way the serpent is all about bad men and the shepherd's daughter is all about woman as saviour.

Life is rarely that simple, and we should not be looking for simple answers here. Best we stew in the whole thing. Own every morsel, stop pushing the salt and grease to the side of the plate.

Seeing Through the Eyes of the Monster

Everything deepens when we look through the eyes of the monster. The serpent.

Do you remember being cold and lonely in the forest as you heard the feasting from the castle? The candles at the window, the gaiety, the laughter. Did you have warmth in your heart for the revellers? I know I didn't.

As a young boy, I failed an exam to go to a school in my town for the supposedly brighter kids. Most of my friends passed, and those friendships ended at that moment. I didn't want them to, they just did. For a time I pined for the imaginary world I thought they were inhabiting – of rarefied conversation and opportunity. Their road seemed clear and shining, mine less so. Far less so. After a time, things changed. And if I witnessed those boys on the road,

I would wish them harm. Misfortune. Craziness. Despair. I wished this upon them. And, in doing so, damaged myself all the more.

Maybe we aren't going to play nice for the first marriage, or second, or third. A wedding like that may work for the castle dwellers but not for a forest being. A being that has been incinerating its prey since it was just days old. That's how it survives. There's a hundred million merciless responses in its nervous system. That won't get wiped out with a few minstrels and a Hollywood soundtrack. So rip and gobble, rip and gobble, rip and gobble.

Samuel Beckett, Frida Kahlo, Alice Oswald and Rainer Maria Rilke, have all stayed loyal to the small, tart seeds of insight that grow from looking through the eyes of the monster.

*T*IME CAME AND THE DAY arrived. She was given the tour – swiftly – by the last remaining servant, and brought into the low-lit room. She glanced at the great, lumbering presence filling half the room. "Ah," she breathed. "You must be my dear husband."

With that she beckoned to the tail to wrap itself around her hips. She smiled, never taking her eyes from the despairing priest, even traced her hand slowly over the scales. Once the ceremony was finished, she turned to the worm: "Dear husband, won't you show me your quarters?"

Even the serpent was surprised. This was not how things had been going.

In the warmth of the hay and secure in his den, the serpent growled: "Take off your nightshirt."

She smiled. "Oh my husband, I want to, truly. Here's the thing. You take off one of your layers of scales, and I'll take off my shirt."

He look puzzled, almost touched. "No one has ever asked me to do that before."

It is a terrible and painful affair to take off a layer of scales.

Finally, he had removed a layer and she took off her shirt, revealing another.

"Take it off," he wheezed.

"Oh I will, if you take off a layer of scales."

Again he spoke wonderingly: "No one has ever asked me to do that before."

You know this dance went on twelve times. Twelve terrible layers.

And underneath? Not a man, not yet. But a kind of blubbery worm, pale and shining.

She did not hesitate.

She took the steel brushes, dipped them
in the ashes and water and took to the skin
of the worm. Now, if you think scale removal
hurts, it is as for nothing as scrubbing the
flesh. He screamed, moaned, pleaded, it took
many hours.

As dawn approached, finally, there was a man
in front of her, with the face of someone sent
into exile a long time ago. Someone with an
ordinary beauty she would love her whole life.
She gently bathed him in the milk as light filled
the dark chamber.

In the morning, when the king and queen
gingerly knocked at the door of the chamber
they saw their son and his beloved happily
in bed together, laughing. Another wedding
was had, a wild, rambunctious affair, a
true celebration, and before too long the
younger brother found his true partner too.
Restoration. It's not too late to long for it,
fight for it, defend it.

In the fields the barley grows a little straighter.
In the river the salmon leaps a little higher.
In the sky the stars glint a little brighter.

From Persona to Presence

It's a fabulous turn in the tale when the young woman reveals such literacy to her situation: "Ah, you must be my dear husband." We sense that somehow, against the odds, she is in command of this incredibly dicey unfolding. Confidence is in abundance; any hesitancy and the old, terrible patterning rears up, the nostrils flare and the serpent breathes fire. It appears that to educate a serpent, you have to show it something it's never seen before, ask it something that no one ever has before. It's a kind of aikido move. The unexpected is key.

She is a well-trained athlete turning up for the main event. Toned and focused. She's diligently engaged with the coming scenario and no doubt faced the serpent of her own fear for this marriage more than once. She's as settled as anyone possibly could be in such a perilous situation.

Imagine a scenario in your own life that has defeated you again and again. Imagine the day when you have accumulated smarts and scar-thick wisdoms to take another tack with it. Suddenly a lock appears and you have the key mysteriously in your pocket. And here we have a clue about how to approach human relationships. How about not *calling your partners on their shit* so much, but *calling them on their beauty*? Their constancy, their courage, their upstandingness. That you don't pulverise, you amplify, you call forth.

As far as I can tell, that's what the scales are about. He can see that she takes him seriously. That she's demonstrably done the work. He's looking at the ornate patterning on the heart-shirts, the nightshirts, and is witnessing real honouring to him and the situation. Suddenly this is no longer a bone-crunching mosh pit but a tango. This is charged, elegant ritual space.

Well, it's elegant till the scales start to come off.

Man or woman, it's a hell of a thing to go through all those layers, layers that have served their purpose. The scales are not necessarily villains in the mix, but things required against the bustle and scuffs of life. I am not a man that believes that all life wishes us well, all the time. I am not a man who believes vulnerability is to be displayed at all times and under all circumstances.

But there may come a day when something so precious arrives that a great deal can fall away. That something essential is both flagrantly visible and then educated. Brought forth. W.B. Yeats drops a few scales in the last years of his poetic life; the very late recordings of Johnny Cash. There is a directness, a learnt simplicity that comes through that contains a greater intimacy than some of the earlier work. Less is more, as the musicians say.

To drop scales is the movement from persona to presence.

As a storyteller it has taken me thousands of hours of public life to drop scales. To profoundly show up. Not as caricature, but me in my own peculiar shape. The belief that I am enough (we will come back to this). Storytelling is a wild way of telling the truth, and the most radical way of doing that is entering any situation with the fullness of your being. You have to have decent footing on your own imagination to be able to do this, to have a mythic ground, no matter how scrappy and humble it is, that you are able to stand upon.

And even then, we're not done. The scrubbing brushes and the baths. An alchemist could give us several hours, at this stage, of all the gradations and varying of temperatures to turn lead into gold. The putrefactions, the fire coaxing – both fierce and timid – separations and comminglings required for such a process. We can see there is pain, even greater pain, at this point. Maybe this is the moment you come to an understanding of quite why those scales were there in the first place.

And if someone is going to use those scrubbing brushes on you, you better damn well trust them.

The water and the ashes are clear-as-day signs of grieving, of the move from pain into appropriate sorrow, into tears, an aquatic flow of release.

And the milk? Well, maybe it is never too late to taste the milk of human kindness. In Devon folklore there's an insistence that a worm can only become a serpent or dragon if it's tasted breast milk. Though there's no image to suggest it, you wonder if the worm caught just a drip before it was flung into the forest. Milk softens, hydrates, nourishes.

The Unspoken Flower: The Black

The anthropologist Victor Turner, drawing diligently from Arnold van Gennep, did a substantial amount of fieldwork on the stages of initiatory process in the Gisu people of Africa in the mid-twentieth century. One of the elements so compelling is those stages being associated with colours: specifically red, black and white. Let's take some of those associations to this story.

> **The Red:** This is a domain of heat, individuation, standing out, making demands. Kill or be killed. You have no problem stating your desire. Fire.
>
> **The Black:** This is a domain of cooling, sobriety, accessing the damage, deepening. Staying one's hand. Ashes.
>
> **The White:** This is a domain of balance, even-handedness, maturity, encouraging others. Raising the culture. Milk.

These colours could arise at differing stages in differing initiations and cultures, but they do tend to show up. The red is 'Older brothers marry first!'; it initiates, doesn't play nice, gets to the front of the line, demands to be heard. It's life force. It's a spark hammering on the anvil of existence; it's red flower all the way. The red is an energy that the West understands and encourages. We could see this most overtly in the first flush of youth.

The black stage generally is later. When you run your finger ruefully over the charred Braille of everything you ever set light to. The black is Underworld knowing, not above-ground smarts. It's counting the cost. There is the slow dawning awareness that you are not going to live forever, that life is brief, that unbridled desire causes consequences. Sometimes in an immature society this causes us to go a little nuts, something frequently named as a mid-life crisis.

The white is later still. Not stuck in the morbidity of black or the hysteria of red, it uses the best of both effectively, and for the good of the whole. You have both life force and experience; you sense advantage but can turn it to more than personal gain. You have a maintained sense of relatedness to the wider world that means your heart is not buried under a tree. You can celebrate others' good fortune. You yourself are milk for others, they come drink from the goodness of your river, you provide shelter under which the exhausted can rest.

I think the serpent was rotting away in the black when devouring the brides, behind the scenes. He couldn't leap from red to white; there must have been some grinding sense of loss. There's a lot of bones in his lair, a lot of blood on the walls. And so when the ritual elder, in this case the young woman, emerges, some part of him is ready for the alchemical grind of real transformative experience.

I think there is a third flower, a black flower, between the red and the white. One the Old Woman never tells us about. A flower only seeded when both are consumed. A flower of life's consequence, and the effort of flourishing within that consequence.

It's the black flower that has the aroma of soul about it. Not just the high spirits of the red, or even-handedness of the white, but the deep material of the black. Not even the Old Woman can tell us how soul kicks in; we have to locate that through necessity of circumstance. It's the stage we are encouraged to avoid. Everyone applauds the brilliant young athlete or the beaming sage, but we skipped something between them. We skipped the story. The whole desperate, ecstatic, raggedy, grace-laden affair. The black flower is also the gold coin we take to the Ferryman as proof we actually incarnated. Stirred up enough trouble with our years.

When the Old Woman tells us of the two flowers – white and red – she is telling us to show up to our own life. The flower she can't show us is what is then born from it. The black. The soul. That we have to find ourselves.

This is a simply extraordinary story. We learn to speak our desire and that desire has consequence, that what we exile must be courted back with beauty, that it must be met with respect, education and imaginative intricacy, and that an alchemy of character is possible when such a journey is undergone. The genius of its framework can be brought into the qualities of our times, and both the squalls and raptures of our private lives. *The Lindworm* is telling us something about how to live.

47

I mentioned earlier that the story itself has a twin. With enough connecting tissue to keep them related, but also distinct in difference, quite radically on occasion. This second story not of exile but of breathtaking proximity to the wild twin: of glee, courage, even true love.

Shall we go?

TATTERHOOD

PINES SURROUND THE
tower, the moat, the ancient seat.

In the snowy north, on a runic scatter of hill and fjord lives a good queen. A good king. No Herods dangling their cherubs, but rivers to their people. Soul-broad. All the right villains are chucked into their chilly dungeons.

And above, in the great hall golden coin falls into the welcome hats of the musicians. These sovereigns can conjure heaven but will plough a furrow with their very fists, if the gods dictate. Their bustling cosmos holds the crouching weaver, the herder, the raw-knuckled fisher people tight in the blue kingdom. All the sheep are gathered in.

But no child.

They are plump with their role, joyous on the royal lanes, but the belly is crow-bare. The

49

leap of the mountain hare is crippled by the
scythe. A scattering of pain webs the ceiling of
these lovers.

The midnight hump becomes dreadful.
The king withers and wipes his shame on the
tapestry. Their grief moves steadily out to meet
the land. Trout turn in the bruise-black streams
and spurt flaccid eggs on the riverbank. The
blond corn loses shape, rots into murk. The fox
shudders with orange fire as it starves.

Someone well meaning offers a delicate
suggestion: why not take a niece for the house?
To flower the corridors with laughing, to loosen
the slow tune of the death fiddle. The sovereigns
listen from beneath their wet bundle of sorrow
and do indeed call such a girl to their service.

The vastness of the castle is hers. The kitchens, the chapel, the sounding-halls where poetic
champions draw from the scarred valleys of
language. Deerhounds her companion, trotting
the gloom. A goodly trouble, she cracks black ice
simply by her kid-swagger, her games, her lovely,
raucous sounds.

She is gifted a ball. A golden ball. Early in
the day she likes to take the ball out to the very
edges of the garden. Where a crusting of forest
waits. Where prim hedges meet the energy of
twig and spell. She loves that place.

It is there she takes her ball, luminous, an axis mundi. She plays all day, cattle-tracks of concentration on her brow, waiting for the dusking time, the mottling light.

Of a sudden, a girl steps forward.

Clear Romany – tilt of head, a-swathed with feather, mucky-footed, delirious and forested.

That golden ball
starts to leap between the two.

From the trimmed grasses to the murk and back again.

A throw like a sighing tide. Farther back in the tree line something watches.

The niece runs to the sovereigns:

"I have news!
I have met a leafy-girl
who says her granny
can make bellies swell
like a browning loaf:

She sings salt back to the ocean
she calls the owl to nestle in the lonely croft
of your hips."

They are summoned.

And the dark stick behind our young one emerges.

Hawk-nosed, thistle-haired, spark-eyed, yolk-fat with cobra-knowledge, pockets a-clatter with

magics, brown fingers dragging rooster blood
from the heart of the moon. In the grandeur of
the hall, at first she denies the powers. That the
child is tongue-eager, bent to exaggeration. But as
the dusk shadows flood over the gold, she relaxes.
In that time before candles are lit, she shows
some form. Her proud shape juts into the room.
She is:

Mearcstapa: the boundary walker
Zaunreiter: a hedge straddler
Hagazussa: hag

She gulps brandy and spits chicken-claw
words:

*"You will never grow large. Your bed is too high, too
smart, too far from dirt.*

*"In your far-off tower, a woman's eggs grow dizzy, a
man's pearling will be as a drizzle of stagnant water.*

*"You can rut like the creamy whale ablaze with its
concubine in the indigo kingdom, but nothing much
will happen.*

*"Take your bed, your pillows that hold your thinking,
your graceful sheets out to the farthest stable with the
pitted earth floor. Tonight, woman, after you bathe,
carry the water, a-clink down the stairs, sloshing with*

your filth. Give it to the stable dirt: four-directioned,
intended, deliberate. Then drag the bed over the pool and
start the steady grind of your seeding.

"At dawn
push the bed aside.

"There will be two flowers —
white and red.

"Eat the white.

"Under no circumstances eat the red.

"Do this and all will change."

Her speaking is strange. Like words gathered
from underneath a stone. By now the
hall is almost completely dark.

As the page lights the first candle, the women
canter out on the dark horses of their pride.

Morning casts golden light through the stable
beams. Bees make rough speech in the furry
meadows. The great bed is pulled aside and there
they are. The white flower eager for the rays, the
red flower sullen, hung over, drunk on privacy.
No one can stop the queen. She squats, all fours,
like a heated bitch, and snaffles up the red.

"My hands made me do it!" comes from the
roughed gob, her tongue still greedily circling
her mouth.

Now the nerves come. She plucks the white
with more canny deliberation, calls her husband
as witness and waits.

In a high tower, nine months have passed.
Ladies jostle to call to the ear the secrets that
a woman needs when she sweats the red gate
between worlds. As a slurry of blood shimmers
her thighs, all hold the image strong of the babe
in health: pink-toed, blue-eyed, cornrow fingers.
Keep thinking it into being.

What bursts through
is not that.

A small goat
hoofs towards the light.
Red-cowled, sticky-furred.

A goat.

And riding its greasy back
is a tiny, hairy baby girl.

A tattered hood
shields most of its face,
hanging limply and dripping.

This deviant, this shape-leaper,
this terror-nymph,
waves a wooden spoon
and gallops the stage,

relishing the screams.

She is appetite; desirous,
hungry for taste, hungry for meat.

She speaks:
"Be patient. Another comes. Twins."
A second later, another gush and a radiance
arrives – a fat sun after horror night. A girl,
beautiful and bawling, cow lashes, grip firm on
the tit. Dawn breaks through the window. The
hairy twin settles in its warmth, beds down on
gathered hay.
And all wonder –
"What to do? What to do?"
Plans besieged the twins as they grew. To
rupture the love between the two sisters. But
wherever they tried to hide the furry one, whatever far distant attic was her nest – her sister
would find her. Energy moves like fast water
between them. As time bangs on, the castle finds
a strange accord with the great awakener.
Her braying intelligence coughs new stories
into the midst of the court. She spills tales
of Moroccan silver and Irish gossip onto the
feasting table, and all know they are the wiser
for it.

The Ball, the Girl, the Old Woman

So, here we are again. A royal couple bent over in obligation but losing something essential to themselves. This is a crisis not of villainy but of good works. Maybe a life of constant charitable acts works for a rare brace of saints and the like, but it seems for us lesser mortals that over-extension can lead to an infertile state, an unseeded field.

This time it is not the queen wandering the forest, but the niece they bring in. And really her love is for the hinge of garden and wood, rather than full immersion. The scene has taken us from the obligations of the grown-ups – the king and queen – into the responsive, reactive world of the young girl. And what does she carry? A golden ball.

Readers of commentary on myth will immediately prick their ears at this point. Much is made of the golden ball. Our great ancestor in all this, Robert Bly, saw it as a gleeful ball of energy that surrounds a child, that we all had one, but as we grew, societal and parental demands for us to behave slowly robbed elements of it, like slices from the whole. Neither us or our beloved could even make up a whole.

So there's a thought that we can see that this is an untampered-with kid. She goes where she wants, follows her nose, rummages around. She's in touch with her curiosity.

If we don't get this in our youth, we may throw our ball when older not to the wild but to the feral. It is not necessarily caught by something that wishes us well. Our golden ball could be caught by a street gang, addiction, untempered coveting, lovers suitably damaged to intrigue us.

Some stories inform us by illustrating wrong turns, others right. This is the latter. This is how it is meant to be. We follow our nose, carry our life force playfully, and strike up relationship with our wild twin early on. And isn't the girl from the forest a kind of twin to the niece of the sovereigns?

Like the sewing of the shirts in *The Lindworm*, the throwing back and forth of the ball soothes us in some way. A focused, flowing exchange between us and the Otherworld. Quite glorious. And who steps forward but the old woman inside the young girl. It could be argued that many of these characters are something like babushka dolls, Russian dolls set inside one another. What activity gave you information beyond your years as a child?

It's also important for us to hold on to the reality that for the tellers of these tales, a wild woman living out in the woods was not a crystallised, metaphorical form, but something that Eastern European cultures would know as a lived experience. They had respected spook about them. Divinatory smarts would be hidden in the folds of such a being's cloak. And yet again, as the centre wobbles, the illumination comes from the edge.

With the brandy and cigars, we see a diminutive mirror of the assembled bards and musicians courting the serpent out of the forest in the previous story. That libation is present. The old woman has plenty to say: that their love-making needs to be closer to the ground, nearer animals, earth, forest. In his extraordinary poem 'The Unfaithful Wife', Lorca breaks into such territory:

> Nor tuberose nor sea shells
> Have skin so delicate,
> Not even mirrors in the moonlight
> Shine with that kind of brightness.
> Her thighs escaped from me
> Like startled fish,
> Half full of fire
> Half full of ice.
> That night I roamed the best of all trackways,
> Mounted on a mare
> Of mother of pearl
> Without bridle or stirrups.

Gentility has frozen them. They need Lorca's seashells, startled fish, fire and ice. And that the queen has to preserve her dirty bathwater. That it has sensual, life-giving energy. We can imagine Janis Joplin and Charles Bukowski happily carrying the water out to the final stable. This time it's not good deeds to others that is going to cut it, but rather attention to your dirt.

Again, descent not ascent. Muck, arousal, passion. She has to get in contact with that. And then real, splendid lovemaking can take place.

Again, the crafty command, 'Whatever you do, don't pick the red flower.'

*A*S THE SECOND DAUGHTER'S body starts to bud, to lift towards woman, winter settles the land with its great flakes of white. There is to be a feast – the first for the fair daughter to emerge, curved and available. Fresh rushes are laid, thick yellow wicks bright the dark corridors.

The father sits alone on the big seat and runs the sharpener against his loyal blade, mind cloudy with worry.

The cluck-strut and stale language of young suitors is a wearied cloak.

It's Christmas Eve.

When all are settled at table, cup lifted, honeyed chop on plate, a groan comes from outside the hall. A keening of many terrible things. From the tree line, and beyond that the lochs and mountain –

Come Witch.

Come Giant.
Come Ogre.
The gaggle-swarm churn up the frosted turf,
shit on the frozen moat, hurling old, black
language at the loafing warriors. Horse-leather
drums thump the occult pace, skulls of snow-
eagles shake atop rowan staffs. The butchers
cower at table.

But the Tattered sister charges the un-killable
throng.

No one blocks her path.

She is swift with the death-screech of the owl.

Fists rain-daggers, her fame a slurry of
violence, hot landed on ghoulish heads. Adrift
in this fury that has greeted them – this tiny
sister, this speck of joyous iron, a grand-general
of malice – the coven scatters, loses its mighty
shape and starts a boozy retreat.

They seem impressed.

Leaning from a window is the bright sister.
Spotted – a witch leans from a foaming mare and
twists her head clean off. From her crane-skin
bag she wrestles a calf's head onto the twitching
body but takes her face as booty, blood-mad
under the braying moon.

This mid-winter surgery has been a success.
The bewildered calf's head squats rough
on the lime-white body. The chambers ring

shrill with a mother's terror; Father grips the confirming walls.

Tatterhood is calm:

"This shape-leap
offers relief.
Rather an animal power close by,
than the violence of unready love
that was being prepared.

"As it goes, I have the sight.
I know where her head will go.

"But two lochs north
there is a longhouse
of Hags.

"The head will be placed on a
rusty nail.

"Me and my calf-sister
will take the foray.

"We will collect,
and with heavy penalty."

The king offers a hundred horseman, a thousand archers, witch-killers, holy sprinklers, coal-souled mercenaries. Beserkers.

The sisters will take none of it but a ship.
The crow caws
that this is for them alone.

One loch then the other. The nested croft of the Blaggard Hags. The harvest is smooth as the Goat-Sister threshes the flesh wall. The head is scooped delicately from that nail. Placed back on rightful shoulders with three flecks silvering the blond.

Decision on the boat. To turn home or the whale-road?

They settle for the vast unfurling, experience's bounty, to reach jubilation, to hang foamy thinking like animal skins from the smoky mast. Three, four years pass this way.

Appropriate Commotion: What Witches Whisper

What ogres came to your door at adolescence? Caused you to set out into life's rougher scrummage? As is often the way, there is a sense of initiatory choreography in this part of the story. Something inevitable is arriving as Tatterhood's sister enters womanhood. Again there is this applied pressure on politeness, this red surge bearing down on the white of genteel society.

But the genteel can be deadly. A salient point is made, something subtle. That the fair maiden is safer with the head of an animal than launched out into the cattle market of political marriage. At the very last moment she has been taken by the old women – the witches – to get smoked in the education of the robust feminine. This seems a most ancient moment.

What did the girl absorb as her head hung on the rusty nail? What stories, songs, jokes and philosophies nestled whispery in her hair and mind? What kind of dreaming did they set about her with, what mythic terrain did she find herself confirmed in? To have the head of an animal for a while is to be thoroughly threshed in the realm of the senses, to witness acute mystery, to behold the blood surge of ancestral history. To enter adulthood without these elements somehow secreted within you is a cultural betrayal.

These days we aren't likely to undergo a period so acutely marked, so precise in its boundaries as the time in the witches' hut, so we often have to personally curate any wisdom when we enter its energy field. This is far from ideal, and far from what I would claim is coherent initiatory practice.

So be it. We can't let that paralyse us, you and I.

We have to retrace our steps. When have you hung in the rich darkness of the hut? What curl of smoky thought wafted up to you? Who got you out? And why does it need to end?

There are some that think it undignified to ask such questions of a story. As if it would break under such enquiry. As someone who asked such questions in prisons, to gang members, to at-risk youth and returning veterans, I say: take your snobbery somewhere else. No part of your attitude is helping the times we're in. It is of life-saving vitality to make connection to a story such as this. It is as complex and philosophically astute as any form of thought you could hope to encounter; it is nothing less than a university of the soul. To repeat: these stories are telling us how to live.

We, most of us, are scrambling around finding fragments of sustenance where we can. We can appear a little freakish from the outside, clutching odd moments of significance from records, books, encounters with the living world. Bricoleurs, ragbag sorts, humble magpies with a few gleaming nuggets of beauty in our nests. Crazy times. But as I said in the introduction to the book, stop and look around yourself again. Attend to the grace. Start to gaze through a divine and subtle lens at your life and everything changes. It doesn't last for long, and the profundity of that realisation can be the beginning of gratitude. Maybe that is what the witches were whispering in the ear of the fair maiden.

These are insights that change the way we behave, the way we choose to steer our boat. Back to the old life, or out on the glitter-green waves. Well, the earth itself is making that decision for us now. There is no safe castle for us to return to; setting out for story is the only thing to do, the only hurl of knucklebones left. Stories that cajole, nibble on the canvas on our sail, jog our compass back into the salty dimensions of our own heart's conscience.

I do not pretend for a moment these are one-size-fits-all replacements for initiations from supposedly exotic, far-off lands. But they are a spirited, gathering-up-skirt harrumph, away from synthetic, glassy-eyed, trance infusions to make young people forget their iridescent feathering, irascible hearts, and delicately hoofed disposition to the mysteries of the world, all of whom are giggling and cheering and flagrantly weeping them on in their spectacular and perfect missteps that charm all magical and secretive things. To a vital and persistent degree we have to labour with what we have, not spit into the dust with ever-lucid bitterness over what we imagine we don't.

By keeping Tatterhood close, the castle is awash with stories. There's been little incineration but an awful lot of delight. But even in the health of such circumstance, we note it was still crucial for the fair maiden to be removed from the domestic. No amount of progressive attitudes and general encouragement can circumnavigate the moment when the initiatory energies must descend.

When I was sixteen I found myself on endless ferry journeys across to Europe to play drums in a punk rock band. I did not find wisdom, but certainly a little excitement. But I was throwing my golden ball to people so damaged they couldn't even catch it. Maybe even recognise it. We, the band, would sometimes have to sleep on the stage of whatever crumbling squat we were appearing in that night, as the party raged on around us. Fights were frequent, drugs were harsh and everywhere and the barometer of any feeling at all was strung out and brutal. The essential resonance was towards a kind of recognition of pain. I longed to be sailing like Tatterhood, but this is what I ended up with. I felt I'd been cheated. I'd forgotten that rock 'n' roll generally eats its young.

But even now, thirty years later, I know what I was setting sail for. I didn't find it. And even now, I can recognise in an instant the initiatory hunger in a young person. For me, it would take living in the shamble-down, broken-down debris of the initiation worth its salt that never actually happened for, magically, something indeed *to* happen. I have built out of my incompleteness. You may be a middle-aged woman and suddenly catch yourself laughing delightedly as you realise that, finally, your head is hanging on that sacred, rusty nail.

There will be worthy types who tell you that's impossible, that such things can only occur in an allotted, youthful time frame, but life is more arcane and generally more unexpected than that. There's just more mischief about than we give credit for.

A DISTANT PORT. A KING IN middle years, widowed – but one who leans into danger. Makes his way through the rigging and gulls to befriend these salty women. His son, with unsung charisma, follows behind.

A love affair erupts between the noble and the fair sister. A horn blows for the marriage binding, but Tatter waves her chafed hand and chants from the greasy hood:

"Older sisters marry first.
Root me with the son —
a double wedding."

Grief-choked, the son and father debate by the long jetty, quietly turning life's forks in their subtle hands. The older shape crumples at the vastness of his son's panache.

Before long three horses and a goat take a flowered lane to the simple chapel.

At the back Tatterhood and the son, her goat's fur stiffened with mud, his horse sure-hoofed, gold bridle and saddle, licked with rubies.

"Why do men never ask the questions that open a woman's soul?" She peers up, curious. "If I tell you what to ask, will you ask me?"

The boy coughs and straightens.

"Certainly."

A true dowry.

"Why do I ride a goat?
Why do I carry a spoon?
Why do I wear a hood?"

"Because for one with eyes to behold it, it's not a goat!"
A Castilian steed rears up.

"Because for one with eyes to behold it, it's not a spoon!"
A rowan wand hums air.

"Because for one with eyes to behold it, it's not a hood!"
A crown of dog rose and antler bone sits aloft.

Bundled hair like dark torrent surges as a
keen sea down the small of her back. Foals
quiver on the green hill. Brandy is drunk from
the Romany's hand. We hear a pipe, a drum, the
rasp of fiddle.

Her beautiful, ordinary face gleams by the
chapel's yellow candle.

The wedding will last for years.

Three Questions

I wonder what it is like to travel for years as the two sisters
do. Accustomed to wealth as they are, this period lasts far
longer than a gap year or extended vacation. They commit. And always heading north. And they meet a grief
man. A king, but a grief man. That's where the journey
leads them. And the first recognition of the maiden with

strands-of-silver-in-hair comes from him. He falls in love with an initiated woman. And where does it lead? To another circling back to the story of *The Lindworm:* "Older sisters marry first!"

We are multitudes. And it appears that everything must marry when one element marries. They didn't marry the same thing – no monotheism there – but the whole den writhes and shudders for their many, complex unions. One affects the many, and out comes the demand for satisfaction.

One of the most exquisite moments in any story I tell are the questions Tatterhood gives her beloved to ask her. She tells him how she needs to be loved. To open up the road into her very soul.

How many of us are either too shy to reveal such questions, or simply so removed from ourselves we don't know what such questions could be? Whatever our age, we should start to speak them. Like the queen in *The Lindworm,* the emphasis is on speaking from our heart and soul.

I hope these stories have ducked and weaved with appropriate style so that they have gathered you in. I don't recommend trying to portray the whole ensemble as a coherent plan, but rather work into the winces and gasps, into the felt, and work out from there.

Sometimes it's a story that shows me what I don't have, rather than what I do, that has me returning over and over.

The story becomes a force field of particular emotion that I most clearly experience there. I lie down beside it, and for a while I may know peace. As Lorca says, in 'Sonnet':

> If you are my hidden treasure,
> If you are my cross and my moist pain,
> If I am the hound of your domain,
>
> Don't let me lose what I have gained
> And decorate the waters of your river
> With leaves from my long estranged autumn.

In the final section of the book we are going to turn to gazing at the time we're in through this mythic lens we are developing. With myth, story and the oral tradition as our companions, what could they be saying about the glory and chaos, the beauty and danger of modernity?

UNDERWORLD
ETIQUETTE

Reevaluate Practical

Let's take a second to consider what we associate with the word *practical*. If we look for its etymology, we quickly run into notions like this:

Practical: from the Greek *practikos* via Latin to the French *practique* and finally to English. Practical is to move from theory to action, words to deeds. Pragmatic, reasoned, useful, applied, utilitarian.

Practical gets up from the table and goes to the toolshed when too many big words are used. It prides itself on a lack of sentimentality; it wants an idea to 'get to the point'. It makes us feel secure in a woefully insecure time. That something can be solved. Practical seems to distrust words. It's a lone rider with the big news. A big problem just needs a big idea. Get thee to thy laptop, measuring tape, bulldozer.

Practical seems the resolute end of whimsy, of nostalgia, of wistfulness. The end of the poet. It does not indulge prolonged bouts of uncertainty or paradox.

But here's the problem. Absolutely the thing. We are utterly beset by both uncertainty and paradox.

Paradox and uncertainty are the acrid tang in the strangulated throat of our times, the very passport to entry, and a whispered, desperate currency amongst our youth. A tool belt can't fix this. Paradox and uncertainty can't be dismissed out of hand. They are the identifying brands of now, our hashtags, our tweets, our sat navs into the murk of consequence.

To a toxic practicality (I think I just invented a phrase) paradox and uncertainty are Scylla and Charybdis – challenges to be outdone (the serpent and whirlpool Odysseus has to navigate) – but to a mythic awareness they cajole new and inventive forms of thought. Please note, I didn't say we enjoy the encounter.

So how's 'practical' working out for us, and what is its relationship to climate change?

Significant, I'd say. Practical in the Western perspective of the word is riven catatonic with limit at this point. Let me just go 'fix' that forest. Improve it. The earth is weary of our practicality.

However, I'm not going to give up on the word entirely, rather view it from the slant.

What would practical look like to an Amijangal elder from the Northern Territory, an Evenk reindeer herder, a Haida stone carver? If the world is thick and credibly teeming with gods disguised as longhorn cattle, weather patterns, even occasionally secreted within conversation, surely a logical, methodical action would be to address them through the ordinary, unhysterical maintenance of prayer, ritual and story? And we know the world over that such beings have a soft spot for beauty.

Real, practical actions are entirely bound up with the business of manners. Yes, you guessed it, courtship.

Humans, as a late form of flowering on the earth, have drained the very life force from the soil-banked world tree of which we are but only one tip. A tip committed to indecent, incessant, lunatic budding. And such a flowering is always the death-signal back to the seed of its origination. And oddly, government response to climate change seems like a tacit suicide bid. I wonder if there is a cultural, not even consciously personal, death wish in the West. Something inside us may simply have had enough. Be disgusted with ourselves. I'll come back to this.

Vigorous industrialisation of countryside then swabbed deep with insecticides, guttering the earth for minerals, withholding vast stockpiles of food while others starve: all of this would have been seen as 'practical actions' to serve the shuffling beast of degraded-human-progress at one point or another. And so many of the diseases that now sluice through our bloodstream and kidneys, livers and guts are but the sorrowing companions of all writ large out there in the gape of lived experience.

Our insides and our outsides are in a face-off. Manners tend to come with the arrival of consequence to our actions. To something up close and likely bringing a little buckle to the knees.

What follows is where I think we are.

As both a mythologist and wilderness rites of passage guide, I am frequently asked to comment about climate change, collapsing stories and what on earth to say to our kids about the future. I am no kind of pundit, so choose my words sparingly and carefully. What follows is a few provocative thoughts.

The real horn being blown at this moment is one some of us simply cannot hear. Oh, we see – the endless television clips of crashing icebergs, emaciated polar bears, and a hand-wringing David Attenborough – but I don't think we necessarily hear. Climate change isn't a case to be made, it's a sound to be heard.

It's really hearing something that brings the consequence with it – 'I hear you'. We know that sensation; when it happens the whole world deepens. If we really heard what is happening around us, it's possible some of it may stop. From a mythic perspective, seeing is often a form of identifying, but hearing is the locating of a much more personal message. Hearing creates growing, uncomfortable discernment. Things get accountable. I worry I have been looking but not hearing.

When I hear, I detect what is being disclosed specifically to me at this moment of shudderation and loss. What is being called forth? Whatever it is, I won't likely appreciate it.

We remember that the greatest seers, the great storytellers, the greatest visionaries are so often blind. Listening is the thing.

In ancient Greece, if you needed wisdom greater than human you went to the market square of Pharae in Achaea and created libation for Hermes, god of communication, messages, storytelling. There stood a statue of the bearded god. After burning incense, lighting the oil lamp, and leaving coin on the right of the deity, you whispered your question in its ear. Once complete, you swiftly turned and left the sacred area with your hands over your ears. Once out, you removed your hands, and the very first words you heard were Hermes speaking back to you. You curated these insights into your heart, pondered and then acted on them. You didn't see Hermes, you heard Hermes. You listened. It's said that in ancient Greece the deaf were shunned through their supposed lack of capacity to hear the gods. That they were spiritually dangerous.

Isn't it interesting that the enquirer to Hermes kept their ears blocked till they were out of the market square, so as not to be assailed by idle, above-world chatter and think it divine? I wonder if we may be asking the question to Hermes but removing our hands too early.

As a storyteller I have noticed when an audience is profoundly absorbing the import of a story; they close their eyes to do so. It deepens the encounter. So anyway, on to my main thought:

I think we are in the Underworld and haven't figured it out yet. Both inside and outside us.

The strange thing about the Underworld is that it can look an awful lot like this one. It's not situated in those esoteric graphs and spiritual maps we study, it's situated as a lived experience.

I recently saw a mist suddenly descend on my garden. It just rolled in out of nowhere. Everything changed, just like that. Very quickly all appeared different, no shrubs, no apple trees, it was a foreign landscape. The dead felt usefully closer, the silence deeper. In just a moment the Underworld seemed present, as an atmosphere rather than concept, a tangible, seasonal shift not a distant idea.

This world can be Otherworld, Underworld, heavenly, hellish and all points in between. It can still be Arcadia, Camelot, Eden almost. That's why it's confusing. We still get to go on holiday, drink wine, watch beautiful sunsets. We still pay insurance and kids still go to college. But there is something happening. An unravelling. A collapsing, both tacit and immense in scale.

We are frightened and we do not know what will happen next.

And into that fraught zone drifts quite naturally the Underworld. This is not the dayworld, this is the nightworld we are entering. The nightworld is not processional, tidy steps and objective outcomes, but potent with insight, uncertainty and the need for dream-skill. The skill is witnessing the depth intelligence that dreams offer, the great plunge into soul's magical disorientations. That's how the earth tends to talk to us, rather than our strip-lit, strip-mined Morse code it has almost been plunged into silence with. It's not the senate that talks with the earth, it's the shaman.

But we are still using dayworld words. This is why so little works.

When we move into Underworld time, mythically the first thing to go is often the lights. This is a shadowed or even pitch-black zone of encounter. Nothing is how it seems on the surface of things. We have to get good with our ears. So to repeat, our eyes alert us to the wider situation, but it's our ears that alert us to the personal, the particular, the micro in the macro. This tends to be when the heart is alerted.

And there's just more of the Underworld about. Its tactile, tangible attributes. We have Penthos (Grief), Curae (Anxiety) and Phobus (Fear), those gatekeepers of the place, roving ever more readily amongst us. Either chronic or acute, acknowledged or not, they are present at our table. So what happens when the underneath, the chthonic, the shadowed material starts to become more and more visible in our lives?

We start to fess up.

The Underworld is a place where we admit our red right hand. We give up the apotropaic.

An apotropaic act is when you ritually ward off evil. When you claim innocence unduly, you are attempting a similar, unseemly act. Keeping your hands clean. So we could entertain our own hypocrisies for a while. That would be suitably sobering. When we start to remove the scaffold of smoke and mirrors propping up our lives, what is left? That is part of an Underworld etiquette.

I also have to say something deeply unfashionable: it is not relentless self-absorption that makes us realise our interior mess is directly mirrored outside ourselves. That's not vanity, that's attention. It's not hubris, it's horrifying clarity. If you don't attend to your soul's vitality with intent, then suppressed it'll run you ragged. They are not above catastrophe to get your attention. Soul seems more dangerous to talk about than sex, violence, death or money these days.

As many nerve endings as there are in a body, are the messages attempting to issue forth amongst place, animal and person in regard to climate change. I think we should forget the rest and attend to ours. Staggering spiritual repair is called for. It is not just those bad white men in power that did this. We all did. Acknowledging that is the end of the apotropaic.

I believe something will crawl back out of the Underworld. It will. It always does. But it may not be us.

The Underworld chews up soundbites, gnaws on the feeble marrow of platitude, pummels certainty or sweeping predictions into the greasy darkness of the cave to gobble later.

The Underworld speaks out of both sides of its mouth.

So being that's where I think we are, I suggest we should develop a little etiquette. Hold a little paradox, to speak out of both sides of our mouths.

An Underworld spirit, either Roman – *di manes,* or Greek – *theoi cthonioi,* doesn't abide in one singular form but several. The one contains the multitude and they have different insights to offer.

I'm going to ask us to hold two, seemingly contrary positions at the same time. That we could deepen into both.

Stop Saying That the Earth Is Doomed

You may be doomed, I may be doomed, the earth not so much.

And anyway, do you have any idea how offensive that is to the gods? To any amount of offended magics? Especially to your children? To the perpetual and ongoing miraculous? In the Underworld, such grand protestations reveal a lack of subtlety. Even hubris.

And who are we, with our unique divinatory access, that we seem to have information withheld from everything else in all time and space. And now, *now* we are suddenly cleaving to the 'facts' of the matter? Facts don't have the story. They have no grease to the wheel, they are often moribund, awkward clumps of information that can actually conceal truth, not promote it.

I'm not even asking for hope or despair, I'm suggesting responsiveness to wonder. To entertain possibility.

And to deepen.

Cut out the titillation of extinction unless we are really prepared to be appropriately stupefied with loss.

To stop trafficking in it just to mainline a little temporary deep feeling into our veins as we post the latest TED Talk on social media. It doesn't mean it's not true, doesn't mean that rivers, deserts and ice floes don't daily communicate their flogged and exhausted missive, but there's an odd twisted eroticism, a Western Thanatos that always comes with excessive privilege. And let's be clear, most of us reading this are excessively privileged. I think some of us are getting off on this. That it-all-will-end inserts some poignancy to a life deprived of useful hardships. Not ever knowing appropriate sacrifice is not a victory, it's a sedative.

But when we prematurely claim doom we have walked out of the movie fifteen minutes early, and we posit dominion over the miraculous. We could weave our grief to something more powerful than that. Possibility.

Let the buck stop with you. Where is your self-esteem if you claim the world is doomed with you still kicking in it? How can that be? What are you, chopped liver? Is that *really* your last word on that matter? I'm not suggesting a Hercules complex land on your shoulders, but if ever you longed for a call to action this is the moment.

Approaching the Truth That Things End

Dancing on the very same spear tip, we accept our very human response to things ending. We don't like it. We loathe it. The good stuff at least. Though it is a historical inevitability, a biological placeholder, could we start to explore the thought that earth may appropriately proceed without us? Without our frantically curated shape? Could our footprints become pollen that swirl up for a moment and then are gone? I'm not suggesting we are anything but pulverised with sorrow with the realisation, and our part in its hastening, but I persist.

I'm offering no spiritual platitudes, no lofty overview, but for once we stop our wrestle with god and feel deeply into the wreckage of appropriate endings. That even, or especially such catastrophic loss requires the most exquisite display of love for what we did not know how deeply we loved till we knew it was leaving.

I think even to operate for a second in the Underworld without being annihilated, we have to operate from both wonder and grief, at absolutely the same time. One does not cancel the other out. It is the very tension of the love-tangle that makes us, possibly, a true human being.

Notice I said approaching, not accepting the truth that things end. That's too swift a move, too fraudulent, too counterfeit, too plastic. Approaching is devastation enough.

This terrible, noble counterweight is what we are getting taught. But it doesn't end there.

There in that very contrariness, something gets forged: something that is neither-this-nor-that, a deepening, ballast in the belly of the ship triality. The blue feather in the magpie's tail, the Hermian move to excruciating brilliance through the torment of paradox, the leap of dark consciousness that we, in the name of culture, are being asked to make. The thunderbolt that simultaneously destroys and creates.

83

These are grand turns of phrase I'm using but I don't apologise. You've been in love once or twice, you know what I'm banging on about.

I once heard that to become a sovereign of Ireland you had to attach a chariot to two wild horses. One would lurch one way, one the other. You revealed your spiritual maturity and general readiness for the task by so harnessing the tension of both that a third way forward revealed itself. The holy strain of both impulses created the royal road to Tara. A road that a culture could process down. I'm talking about something like that. That's Underworld character.

And such sovereigns were not defined by what they ransacked, what they conquered, but how they regulated their desire, how they attended to the woes and ambitions of their steeds for a third way to reveal itself. Under great pressure and with immense skill.

The nightworld is where we are.

I say it. I say it till we may hear it.

And in that darkness, we remember what we love the most.

That itself is the candle.

So my next piece of practical action is to get clear on your care.

What Do You Love?

Recently I spent an evening with a group of academics and students, talking about reaching out to the earth. They were in complete agreement that eros was the bedrock relationship to all living things. That sensual, tingling, vivacious connection. This was a big hit with everyone. You felt it. That you trusted your senses and took pleasure in them. I think we all like this idea. What's wonderful is that it brings us utterly into the present moment, without a scientist or guru or preacher to interpret. As many have noted, religion is often a wonderful defence against having a religious experience.

But this is my caution. Addiction only to eros is the end of loyalty to person or place or community. One evening you will wait up but find no nightingales under your window. Because it's Amor the nightingales come for, not Eros. It has specificity. Eros can't be the whole story. If it was, we could just squat down anywhere and open to its sensual enfoldings. For most of us, that can't work. Some places claim us, some don't. Like people. Just as sex without love eventually exhausts us, constant transmogrification through landscape after landscape can become thin, exhausting and in the end superficial.

Openness to all can be the end to loyalty to anything in particular. That everything is freighted just the same.

But myth rarely traffics in such equality. I think many of them are infused with amor. They are a love letter to a very specific bend of river where the salmon run in a blue-smoked Connemara autumn, or a crest of Devon granite tors forged from combat between Arthur himself and a powerful west country spirit. As Tom Waits once said, somewhere: "A song needs an address."

Every land-spun detail is an ivory comb through the mane of the story, is a tenderness, a remembering, an intimacy. That maintains a potent charge between human and earth, that in its fullness could be called a songline. That we pine when we are away from it.

Amor brings heart-sickness, not just libido. But that very sickness can have discernment at its core. I want to defend it. We rarely fight for an abstraction, not necessarily even our country; we fight for our regiment, or the village or the home. Our kids. This specificity and its ensuing heart-sickness is not a weakness but an indicator. It provokes what we stand for, how we earn our name; it can flare up enormous acts of courage in its wake.

I can witness the almost hallucinatory glory of prairie and Pacific, but my feeling-relationship with Britain is entirely different. I have been claimed by certain stretches. I can't just bounce from ecstasy to ecstasy across the world. Flower to flower to flower makes you a gigolo, not a husband.

The Underworld wants to make a husband of you. A wife. A being of fidelity, wherever you are on any spectrum.

Speak to Our Times in the Way It Best Understands

So I've suggested listening as a practical action. I'm now going to move to speech. If you actually carry a few ancient stories in your jaw, then the very words themselves are how you taste your ancestors, how you most dynamically inhabit the roughage and complexity of their thoughts. By passing them on. They have travelled thousands of years to take up location in the pearly palace of your mouth.

As we walk through the darkness with the candle of our love, we should speak in language the Underworld understands. We should speak with story.

A note: I am sympathetic to those who feel that storytelling – the *stand-up-and-do-it* variety – is simply not for them. It is a very particular art, I understand that. It halted me in my tracks for years and years. But if you are still reading this book, then I can only surmise you have some interest in, even love for myth and its relationship to the earth. For those in that particular part of our collective cave, I'd ask you to continue reading and see what you could adapt into some other art form. That kind of wiliness is a needed ability right now. I'm going to walk through several points towards myth telling in the way I understand it.

You Are Enough

This is the major, deadly, ice-riven mountain to traverse. That you, yourself, are enough. Most of us don't feel even nearly enough to stand up and tell a story. Mark Rylance has been saying the same thing with actors for years, the essential truth so hard to absorb. That we, in our incompleteness, jagged and nagging doubts, occasionally

far-too-loud voice and woefully bad hair, may have some
kind of truth to articulate. That only we can. And that
for a moment that little truth finds itself in the larger,
purring, ornately arrayed beast that is a myth.

The audacity required. The shamelessness. The guts.
I remember being both hypnotised and acutely dismayed
when I used to go and watch the Scottish storyteller Robin
Williamson. It was like witnessing a lordly hallucination
emerging directly from my own florid imagination of
quite what the glory of words could conjure. His eloquence, the leaping wit, the gravitas, the sheer wingspan
of his material: from epic to yarn to folktale and back
again. The humility with which he so lightly carried it all.
There was no one remotely like him. And, of course, like
so many of us do in life, I measured myself against him,
and found myself appropriately lacking.

I'm not that spiritually evolved, so all real news tends to
create a sense of dismay in me. I was both delighted Robin
existed and paralysed with shame at the deficit of my own
character and abilities. And so this continued. The first
key chucked into my self-created prison cell was lowering
my expectations, and approaching a more modest endeavour than somehow mastering his entire repertoire; in fact
I wisely left it completely alone. I simply learnt a Russian
fairy tale, probably three pages in length. I whispered it
out in several fairly benign environments before gradually
upgrading to an audience of three. And so it remained.
For hundreds of hours live it remained that way. I played

a pattern on a drum underneath, entirely for the security that if I forgot the story I could play till it shuffled back into my memory. I remember the night, three years into telling stories, that I finally slammed my hand down on the drum skin, got up, and walked to the other side of the drum. Exposed.

I could fill the remainder of the book with moments like these, but the point is that stories were waiting all along for me to show up with my whole self. That's what they require. More than winged eloquence, more than staggering displays of memory, more than recited lists of slaughtered warriors, they want to see you there. All of it. To be settled in the bone-house of yourself.

Take courage. Do the work. Don't go easy. And know this, you have more of the stuff than you will ever need.

Your Life Is What the Gods Create Their Stories From

We learn something very important in Irish myth: that the stories told in the Otherworld have us as the main characters. When the Fairy, the Benji, the Sidhe, the hedgerow ancients, when even the Gods and Goddesses of Beyond Old Time Altogether gather by the embers, it is your story, it is my story, they speak of. So, if nothing else, let's give them something to talk about. And the clearer you are about its twists and turns, sudden nips to the ankles, succulent slobbers on fruit from gods' own gardens, then the better they hear the story. And to be clear, they don't just need drama, that doesn't necessarily impress them.

They want to see the kind of sacrifices that all adults make for their kids, the trading of growth for depth sometimes, to live with less so that the wider herd flourishes. The more we cut out the lies, the more we delight them. There are many more eyes upon us that wish us grace than wish us harm.

Myths Are Robust

Okay, here's a secret I don't say very often. Myths are not only to do with a long time ago. They have a promiscuous, curious, weirdly up-to-date quality. They can't help but grapple their way into what happened on the way to work this morning, that video that appalled you on YouTube. Well, they are meant to; if they didn't they would have been forgotten centuries ago.

The rule – and there is one – about old stories is that you can add a flavour here and there, but don't change the recipe completely. If you cut and paste stories together, the ancestral heft tends to drop out of the endeavour and you are left oddly weightless. Possibly charming, likely inventive, but without that deep, slowly, slowly marinated power that endless tellers laboured diligently and delightedly over before you or I turned up. So get from A to Z, but keep alive to what you have seen on the way. That's where your particular genius rocks up, your artistry in fact. It's this balance between tradition and innovation that is so compelling when working itself out in the nervous system of a storyteller right there in front of us.

Now theatre, literary mythic fictions, one-person shows, dance pieces: that's a wider scope I admire but don't know much about. My muttered advice here is for anyone who is interested essentially in solo, oral telling with a strong component of psychic weight.

More practical action: if a story is animate, then remember to feed it. It'll get peckish. It's not merely a set of symbols, a brocade of allegories, a well-positioned teaching tale; it is an energy field. A field that you are now walking with. The oldest and, dare I say, most magnificent art form of them all. So appropriate respect is due.

Dress well when you tell. Leave good grub and fine wine in some secretive part of your apartment or garden. Invite it to speak to you in your dreams. Build it a small hut to reside in when resting from living on your tongue. Don't tell too many other stories in too close a period in case you hurt its feelings. Keep showing up for it.

Learn to wait. Stories will wait years for your thinking to catch up with theirs. Stop plundering Google and pay attention to the stories that keep lurching up in others' conversations. The fairy tales that hang whispy-like to their sufferings and occasional glories.

Again, learn to wait. Some stories want a decade of your time, just to know you're serious.

Place: Love It the Way It Wishes to Be Loved
As Gary Snyder says: "Be famous for five miles." Attend your ear to the gossip of local folklore, plant life, the

myriad ways people blurt, croon and whisper to one another and the wider world. William Blake found much of what he needed in London, with burning bushes and fiery choirs round certain street corners. While I am raising the bar rather high with Blake, what I'm really suggesting is becoming a cultural historian of place. I wrote a whole book, *Scatterlings,* about this very thing.

Central to that book was the distinction between being 'from' a place and 'of' a place. You could become 'of' a place quite late in life. It's not to do so much with the bones of your ancestors in the grounds, or a many generational-spanning lineage; it's to do with a dynamic, psychoactive relationship that arises between the two of you. It's not addressing the pigment of your skin or the inner salutations of your religion; it's more mischievous than that. It's the amor thing I just wrote about. Never too old to fall in love.

And as with love, a great preservative to its continuance is finding out the way the place wishes to be loved, not the way you wish to love it. That's going to involve diligent listening, repetitious acts and an ever-deepening devotion. There is an inevitability that some of us will live lives situated in differing locations. The health of that is on a case-by-case basis, but in many situations I understand it. But what I recommend, over and over, is diligent listening.

Be Sceptical of the Quick Route

Underneath a motorway there was once a road, underneath the road there was a lane, underneath the lane there was a track and underneath the track there was once an animal path. Hoof prints under the concrete. It is the animal path that wants to walk you back into the ready receivership of contact with your own soul. Very, very little in this book is encouraging the allure of the swift.

There's not much in today's more audacious predicaments that doesn't grumble around the pathological desire to get anywhere as quickly as possible. It would be an extraordinary act of will and beauty to check that in ourselves. To question it. Not with pious, judgemental intent, but with a desire to remember the sheer worth of things. Part of the insidious and growing meaningless many experience is the fact that speed is not bringing substance. Its very ease derails us from the capacity to understand the process of making. A woven bag, a diligently apportioned novel, the tanning of a hide, these things really take time. Long after the initial euphoria of the task has gone.

There's something akin to a tantrum in many of us when we don't get what we are accustomed to, immediately. There's a clue in that. Tantrums are for toddlers, not adults. That finger-snapping routine is a childish mode, not befitting someone who is cooked in the presence of much that has fallen away.

At the risk of undue simplicity, this very impetus has got to be behind the incessant castration of the earth. A blight on multitasking. There, I said it.

Be aware that the hour is late. Much is falling away. And that anything still alive in these enormous transitions is shouting to everything else that may possibly be alive. Mythologies are commingling and attempting to reform at lightning speed. And that though many stories are place-specific, some stories have a migratory agency and are designed to travel. They need to be welcomed. Ponder what are the home-making skills required to welcome such a story? The story will likely be powerful, disorientated and requiring shelter. Amongst all the plastic and garbage the sea is washing up, things are arriving on our shore that we desperately need to know about. These are not usually mythologies arriving, but fragments, little broken-off stories, potent but propelled into their own kind of liminality rather than resting in the wider den of an established mythos. We have no idea if they will wither or flourish, but quiet attention is a gift we could give them. See what it wants to say. Some call this a Hermes era, due to the speed of communication, but there is a specific tone to journeys of the winged god: he communicates from soul to soul. If the soul is not open, then Hermes is not present. Remove the flowers and the bee is taskless. We have information aplenty, but do we have meaning? Though it may not be quite clear yet, in the barrage of statistics and general bad news, these stories bring fragments of meaning in troubled times. Like Psyche, we can separate out the grains of their insight in the half-light.

Rescue the Third Thing

Strange as it may seem, couples planning to marry sometimes come to me for advice. I tell them to go study a magpie together, and not to return till they've figured out why I've asked them to do this. This is usually the last I see of them. But for the ones who do return, they always bring the same insight: that amongst the black and white feathers they glimpsed a blue feather. For a couple to survive in the pressure cooker of the home, a third position is vital to the warring polemics that comes in any argument. That we make a nest for a possibility that is more than just right and wrong. To take myth seriously we need a blue-feather language. That's what it can offer us. The immense sophistication of its images will tune conversations to a far deeper dimension than the steady drill of statistical misfortune or hand-wringing guilt. Myth is a shield within whose reflection we can view Medusa. If we keep staring head-on into the abyss, we will have not artfulness but burnout. Much nimble language has simply been thrown away in the search for soundbites; let's rescue it. Neruda is needed in the House of Commons.

So attend to what isn't getting said in a conversation. Listen for the absence and speak to it. It will not fail you.

It may not be comfortable, but so little of what's good for us is.

Twelve Secret Names

I have not had a conventionally easy life. I have eaten a lot of failure and been dealt heartbreak. I have spent long stretches of it having to make friendship with myself because I am often alone. There's no plea attached to that, it just is. And in middle age I can't remember if I am responding to the aloneness or creating it from necessity. But there it is, my old compadre. My dear, dear friend now. I won't be meeting aloneness of a sudden, at the end of life, or widowed; here it is right now. I have lived with little money for long, long stretches, betrayed others and been walloped myself in just the same way. I have been in most positions on love's sometimes infernal wheel of desire and loss. I have followed many false trails and been fairly eaten alive with envy and the acidic hiss of rage for decades at a time. I have been fallen, I have been lesser, have truly wallowed in the mud of life's low thump. I have been unripe, violent and aroused by conflict.

As I have aged, I assess myself more by what I was able to put down for the good of others than by what I have amassed. I remain incomplete, I understand lack, I cook slowly in the horse dung of its wisdoms. I think this is an appropriate position for me at least.

All of these things have made me a more than decent storyteller.

Years ago I heard about something called an *I Am* poem. It was an old Celtic thing, the kind of missive you would have hewn onto a breastplate or shield:

I am the crow that picks at your bones
I am the glory of the green stream
I am the god walked clear from the sun

But tell me, isn't that just another form of domination-speak? More endless, clashing, claiming of ground? The philosopher John Moriarty always said it was. Ah, well again, he was of those spiritually evolved fellows. Myself, less so. I thought it was magnificent, a clatter-bash of words if ever you were in trouble. I loved the amplification, the audacity, the writ-largeness of the thing just so you could, for a second, glimpse yourself more clearly.

The problem was, when I attempted to daub my own blue words on my shield, thread such flowering language on the horns of my word-cattle, not much could come. Not much but damage. I spoke a damaged language.

But still, I longed for relatedness. The back-and-forth of the thing. The affectionate affinities, the deathly hard-won totems. All I could bring forth was my rosary of sorrowing. And that was all right. To the curlew and the willow by the tent I lived in, that was all right.

Let go your big bold banter
Your tongue gives a charring

Not a night jar blessing
It's all right, it's quite alright

Years passed in the tent. Rain over the valley, visits from friends, hammering and banging and coaxing and pleading for the fragrance of place to have just a little action in my vowels and burrs and boasts. No phone pulsed in my pocket, no laptop sat on my desk. I would dream of becoming ghost. And still no *I Am* poem. There still is no *I Am* poem.

So one day, when I was less of myself, I took a walk. And suddenly I seemed to see secret things, hidden things. I beheld them. I saw a beech was only a beech because someone told me it had that name. In fact, these great characters had attributes quite different to one another, and I found myself on this particular afternoon quietly naming out loud the things that didn't unite them but made them individual from one another. Quite naturally and organically I would get to twelve and find myself done. I would take myself to the cool, majestic skin-bark of the being and whisper the names.

The sensation was not of dictating names but of beholding names. Of a ground-down receptivity to what is, not what I hoped was. When I woke the next day, it was an accommodating universe blazing up before me. Just like that. All I had to do was to quieten down and listen to what was wishing to announce itself. If I'd known the word at the time I may have witnessed it as a kind of phenomenology of the soul, but I just called it beholding.

Years later I would find that naming moving towards anything that I detected the appropriate echolocation from.

In these times, is it not the moment to stop telling the earth what it is and what its fate will be? Is it not time to start beholding not dictating? There is some particular constellation of relatedness that will befit you almost as a cosmology if you give it the requisite attention: between animals, weather, nature, the maturity and irascibility of your character, you will constellate. This is not a florid aspiration, this, in a mad and fractured time, is getting glimpse of substantial ground.

Go looking for your beloved. Seek them out, attend to them and give words away with no thought of personal advantage. Be like Robin Hood in this regard. The earth may be hurting, bewildered, furious beyond comprehension, but lower your gaze a little, find some small pocket you love and settle until they have something they wish to whisper to you. The old stories are a currency they understand, adore even, because occasionally they hear their own voices speaking back to them.

If there is anything in this book or my wider work that speaks to you, attracts you, intrigues, infuriates or beguiles you, it means we have what they used to call *rapport*. That's a proper, Old World romance type of language. The reason I say it is that it means the final nesting place for this dialogue is with you, your shape, your discipline, your character, your work. If you didn't have an essential accommodation of these wild ideas yourself you simply wouldn't still be reading. The sheer identification of your interest, or your page turning, means that something is stepping forward to articulate itself within you. Something I know nothing about, but I'm damn excited it's happening.

This is not blowing smoke up your derrière, this is not self-help, this is not bland statements of affirmation, this is something quite focused I'm saying. If you hear anything in this book, hear this:

You are not here to be anything that you want, you are here to be something quite specific.

The gods and goddesses of passion *and* the limits of passion can help you in this regard. Don't go back to sleep. Remember what I said at the very beginning of this odd little book. Relatedness. In revulsion of the shortcut I have taken a long route to, it is hoped, articulate some of the appropriate price attached to such coherent attention. What you want is going to take time. You and I and the whole culture around us need to get conscious on not just the red and white flowers, but the black. As we enter the Underworld, story with its nightworld potency is the great and painful articulation of our deepest character. Myths are a secret weapon. A radical agency for beauty in the age of amnesia. An agency far beyond concept and polemic.

> *May you always be fertile at the centre of your*
> *kingdom. If you fall to fallow as we sometimes*
> *must, may you meet the old woman of the*

forest. May you meet the serpent and the crossroads. May you hear the music when your people call you back. May you be lucky enough to meet educated hearts when you do. May the bath of milk soothe the rawness of your flayed skin.

May you meet your tattered twin. May you never forget her perfume, his laugh, their genius glee.

May you encounter all the appropriate trouble, sail north, always north, as stories fall like snowflakes on your deck. May you be a worthy candle in this world, not too brash, but of the deep light that illuminates where resting animals lie in fresh hay under green boughs that god's own owls hoot from. May you defend what you must, don't go easy, and enter the great longhouse of your people when your time comes. Your people will be singing. May the fire be lit for you, white gold on your fingers, hounds by your feet, wine for your cup, blessed food for your plate.

What are the twelve secret names of that which claims you?

Start there and radiate out.

THE STORIES

THE LINDWORM

OH THERE WAS A KINGDOM
of curlews and inkberry, snowy mountain
and tangled byre, a kingdom of bristling meadows and secretive pools of water only you know
about. The hawk circled such pools, and fish
darted swiftly under the surface.

In the centre of the kingdom presided a king
and queen. Gracious and attentive to their people, distributors of favours, settlers of disputes,
throwers of banquets, you never heard a bad
word about them. But at night a sorrowful grief
hung between them. They could not conceive a
child. This nibbled away at the queen, slowed
her every step, and so she took herself off to the
surrounding forest, hoping a stroll would calm
her anguish.

Under the bough of an oak tree she met
an old woman, who recognised the tension

in the young woman's face. When the queen
unburdened herself of her concern, the crone
claimed she had a remedy for the issue, and if
she followed her instructions exactly, then all
would be well. She spoke:

"You need to give voice to what you truly
desire. Get your breath on it. Tonight at dusk,
walk to the north-west part of the garden
and, as you go, speak everything you wish to
see arise. Finally, speak the last words into a
double-handled cup, flip the cup onto the dark
soil and go to bed. In the morning there will be
two flowers under the cup. One red, one white.
Eat the white, but under no circumstances the
red. Eat the white and you will have that which
you cherish the most."

At the end of the day, the queen did just that.
She strolled and spoke, whispered and crooned
everything that was in her heart. Gave every
fissure of longing voice, then blew into the cup
and flipped it onto the soil. That night she made
love with her husband.

In the morning she walked to the cup and
turned it over. Just as the old woman had said:
the red and white flower. She remembered
exactly the instructions of the crone.

Ah, why do we do this?
Why do we do this?

Why do we do this?

Before she knew it she was on all fours gobbling up the red flower, every last bit of it. In the doing of it, her body rang out like a struck bell of rapture. Every nerve ending accomplished itself in an exfoliation of ecstasy.

And then, slowly, she came back to herself. This wasn't what the old woman suggested. In fact it was the opposite of what she suggested. Guiltily she reached for the white flower and consumed it. She and her husband made a decision – no one needed to know – it was settled.

Well, the old woman's magics worked; she immediately felt new life nibbling at her energy and nine months later she went into labour. A centre that had been barren was about to demonstrate its fertility again.

The strangest thing happened: it was not a child that exclaimed itself from the queen's womb but a small black snake, a worm. Such was the shock of the moment, the midwife grabbed the writhing serpent and hurled it far out of the window into the darkness of the forest. Only minutes later a baby boy was born, and the snake was forgotten, never to be spoken of.

Years passed and the boy became a young man. A man that wished for a wife, a love, a companion. And that sort of thing requires searching for; it requires a quest. He went to his parents, and they gave him permission to travel out and see if such a one existed. They gifted him a white horse and white saddle and bridle for the occasion.

Such high spirits as he galloped from the castle, heart a-rat-a-tat-tat in his chest.

Farther he went into the forest, past the typical hunting spots he had enjoyed, far deep into the dreaming. He came to a crossroads, and it was there that his life utterly changed.

Rearing up before him was a huge, scaled, black serpent. Steam from its nostrils and a raw bellow from its snapping jaw: "Older brothers marry first! Older brothers marry first!"

Sensibly, the young man fled, but for the rest of the day every crossroads he came to there was a serpent bellowing: "Older brothers marry first!"

Exhausted, shaken, he returned to his parents that night with a question:

"Is there anything about my birth that may have slipped your mind to tell me? Anything involving a furious black snake that claims to be my older brother?"

His parents went blank at the query. We don't know if they recalled or not. Whether they were stalling or innocent of memory. What we do know is that all three of them visited the midwife and asked her the same question. By now such a tiny woman she could have taken residence in a matchbox, she finally spoke: "No, no, no, no, no, yes, no, no, no, no." They heard that *yes* secreted amongst the *no*s, and suddenly she was adrift in confession.

"Well. I don't quite like to recall, but yes, maybe definitely there was a wee black worm that shot from the queen. A terrible-looking thing. I held it for a fraction of a second then hurled it into the dark and the rain. And now look at you, handsome prince, why bother thinking of a little freak like that when we can enjoy you?"

The family went very quiet. But it was a useful kind of a quiet, a deepening, and from that deepening something extraordinary was hatched. The king spoke:

"If it is true that this is your brother, then we must not send hunters into the forest to slaughter it. We must send the poets, the musicians, the storytellers to court it from its lair. It needs to be with us. It needs to come home. We need to make a home for the serpent."

And that was exactly what happened. In the belly of the castle, a room was filled with hay to make a vast nest, and slowly, through kind words and lively music, the black snake slouched towards its family. It was so vast the doors had to be widened to get him in; tapestries got scorched by his breath. But by the end of the month, it had happened: the snake was in residence.

And from the centre of the castle, all heard the bellow:

"Older brothers marry first!"

They messaged all corners of the land: 'dark prince seeks bride', and the response was keen. One of the applicants was confirmed and brought to the castle. After a tour of the grounds, she was taken into a low-lit room with a priest. A vast, dark presence filled half of it. As she repeated the vows, a scaly tail wrapped itself around her legs and hips three times. In the morning there was nothing but bones in the hay, and a worm calling: "Older brothers marry first!"

You can be sure that after a few more applicants, the position took on less glamour, and rumours started to circulate. It was 'the castle you went into and never came out'. The messengers still circulated, but for a few months everything went quiet. Even the rats were leaving the cellars of the place, let alone the servants. Albatross albatross albatross. Mary Celeste.

With this in mind, it was a big surprise when a message came through from the daughter of a shepherd. That she would marry the prince, but wished for a year and a day to prepare herself.

The shepherd had heard the rumours and was distraught at his daughter's decision. She herself was not quite sure why she'd made it. As always in times of unrest, she took herself to the woods to think things through, feel things through.

As she sat under the shade of an oak bough, an old woman walked clean out of the tree. Not round the tree, not towards the tree, out of the tree.

For the second time in our tale, an old woman offered instruction:

"It was a brave thing to take this on, but wiser still to give yourself time to figure out a plan.

"If I was you, if I was you, if I was you, I would sew twelve nightshirts for your wedding night.

"Embroider especially around the heart. I would insist that one bath of water and ashes was prepared, and one of milk, and two great scrubbing brushes supplied. The baths and the brushes are to be left in the bed chamber. And quite what do you do with this advice? Well, that's what the rest of your preparation time is to figure out." And with that she walked back into the core of the tree.

For the rest of her time, the young woman laboured on the shirts. She'd never worked with that kind of intricacy before, and her hands ached and fingers got pricked by the needle. But she worked on, educating herself in both delicacy and stamina, persistence and imagination. She thought about quite what it was she was marrying, and how to approach such a thing.

Time came and the day arrived. She was given the tour – swiftly – by the last remaining servant, and brought into the low-lit room. She glanced at the great, lumbering presence filling half the room. "Ah," she breathed. "You must be my dear husband."

With that she beckoned to the tail to wrap itself around her hips. She smiled, never taking her eyes from the despairing priest, even traced her hand slowly over the scales. Once the ceremony was finished, she turned to the worm: "Dear husband, won't you show me your quarters?"

Even the serpent was surprised. This was not how things had been going.

In the warmth of the hay and secure in his den, the serpent growled: "Take off your nightshirt."

She smiled. "Oh my husband, I want to, truly. Here's the thing. You take off one of your layers of scales, and I'll take off my shirt."

He look puzzled, almost touched. "No one has ever asked me to do that before."

It is a terrible and painful affair to take off a layer of scales.

Finally, he had removed a layer and she took off her shirt, revealing another.

"Take it off," he wheezed.

"Oh I will, if you take off a layer of scales."

Again he spoke wonderingly: "No one has ever asked me to do that before."

You know this dance went on twelve times. Twelve terrible layers.

And underneath? Not a man, not yet. But a kind of blubbery worm, pale and shining.

She did not hesitate.

She took the steel brushes, dipped them in the ashes and water and took to the skin of the worm. Now, if you think scale removal hurts, it is as for nothing as scrubbing the flesh. He screamed, moaned, pleaded, it took many hours.

As dawn approached, finally, there was a man in front of her, with the face of someone sent into exile a long time ago. Someone with an ordinary beauty she would love her whole life.

She gently bathed him in the milk as light filled the dark chamber.

In the morning, when the king and queen gingerly knocked at the door of the chamber they saw their son and his beloved happily in bed together, laughing. Another wedding was had, a wild, rambunctious affair, a true celebration, and before too long the younger brother found his true partner too. Restoration. It's not too late to long for it, fight for it, defend it.

In the fields the barley grows a little straighter.
In the river the salmon leaps a little higher.
In the sky the stars glint a little brighter.

TATTERHOOD

PINES SURROUND THE
tower, the moat, the ancient seat.

In the snowy north, on a runic scatter of hill and fjord lives a good queen. A good king. No Herods dangling their cherubs, but rivers to their people. Soul-broad. All the right villains are chucked into their chilly dungeons.

And above, in the great hall golden coin falls into the welcome hats of the musicians. These sovereigns can conjure heaven but will plough a furrow with their very fists, if the gods dictate. Their bustling cosmos holds the crouching weaver, the herder, the raw-knuckled fisher people tight in the blue kingdom. All the sheep are gathered in.

But no child.

They are plump with their role, joyous on the royal lanes, but the belly is crow-bare. The leap of the mountain hare is crippled by the scythe. A scattering of pain webs the ceiling of these lovers.

The midnight hump becomes dreadful. The king withers and wipes his shame on the tapestry. Their grief moves steadily out to meet the land. Trout turn in the bruise-black streams and spurt flaccid eggs on the riverbank. The blond corn loses shape, rots into murk. The fox shudders with orange fire as it starves.

Someone well meaning offers a delicate suggestion: why not take a niece for the house? To flower the corridors with laughing, to loosen the slow tune of the death fiddle. The sovereigns listen from beneath their wet bundle of sorrow and do indeed call such a girl to their service.

The vastness of the castle is hers. The kitchens, the chapel, the sounding-halls where poetic champions draw from the scarred valleys of language. Deerhounds her companion, trotting the gloom. A goodly trouble, she cracks black ice simply by her kid-swagger, her games, her lovely, raucous sounds.

She is gifted a ball. A golden ball. Early in the day she likes to take the ball out to the very edges of the garden. Where a crusting of forest waits. Where prim hedges meet the energy of twig and spell. She loves that place.

It is there she takes her ball, luminous, an axis mundi. She plays all day, cattle-tracks of concentration on her brow, waiting for the dusking time, the mottling light.

Of a sudden, a girl steps forward.

Clear Romany – tilt of head, a-swathed with feather, mucky-footed, delirious and forested.

That golden ball
starts to leap between the two.

From the trimmed grasses to the murk and back again.

A throw like a sighing tide. Farther back in the tree line something watches.

The niece runs to the sovereigns:

"I have news!
I have met a leafy-girl
who says her granny
can make bellies swell
like a browning loaf:

She sings salt back to the ocean
she calls the owl to nestle in the lonely croft
of your hips."

They are summoned.

And the dark stick behind our young one emerges.

Hawk-nosed, thistle-haired, spark-eyed, yolk-fat with cobra-knowledge, pockets a-clatter with

magics, brown fingers dragging rooster blood
from the heart of the moon. In the grandeur of
the hall, at first she denies the powers. That the
child is tongue-eager, bent to exaggeration. But as
the dusk shadows flood over the gold, she relaxes.
In that time before candles are lit, she shows
some form. Her proud shape juts into the room.

She is:

Mearcstapa: the boundary walker
Zaunreiter: a hedge straddler
Hagazussa: hag

She gulps brandy and spits chicken-claw
words:

*"You will never grow large. Your bed is too high, too
smart, too far from dirt.*

*"In your far-off tower, a woman's eggs grow dizzy, a
man's pearling will be as a drizzle of stagnant water.*

*"You can rut like the creamy whale ablaze with its
concubine in the indigo kingdom, but nothing much
will happen.*

*"Take your bed, your pillows that hold your thinking,
your graceful sheets out to the farthest stable with the
pitted earth floor. Tonight, woman, after you bathe,
carry the water, a-clink down the stairs, sloshing with*

your filth. Give it to the stable dirt: four-directioned,
intended, deliberate. Then drag the bed over the pool and
start the steady grind of your seeding.

"At dawn
push the bed aside.

"There will be two flowers —
white and red.

"Eat the white.

"Under no circumstances eat the red.

"Do this and all will change."

Her speaking is strange. Like words gathered
from underneath a stone. By now the
hall is almost completely dark.

As the page lights the first candle, the women
canter out on the dark horses of their pride.

Morning casts golden light through the stable
beams. Bees make rough speech in the furry
meadows. The great bed is pulled aside and there
they are. The white flower eager for the rays, the
red flower sullen, hung over, drunk on privacy.
No one can stop the queen. She squats, all fours,
like a heated bitch, and snaffles up the red.

"My hands made me do it!" comes from the
roughed gob, her tongue still greedily circling
her mouth.

119

Now the nerves come. She plucks the white
with more canny deliberation, calls her husband
as witness and waits.

In a high tower, nine months have passed.
Ladies jostle to call to the ear the secrets that
a woman needs when she sweats the red gate
between worlds. As a slurry of blood shimmers
her thighs, all hold the image strong of the babe
in health: pink-toed, blue-eyed, cornrow fingers.
Keep thinking it into being.

What bursts through
is not that.

A small goat
hoofs towards the light.
Red-cowled, sticky-furred.

A goat.

And riding its greasy back
is a tiny, hairy baby girl.

A tattered hood
shields most of its face,
hanging limply and dripping.

This deviant, this shape-leaper,
this terror-nymph,
waves a wooden spoon
and gallops the stage,

relishing the screams.

She is appetite; desirous,
hungry for taste, hungry for meat.

She speaks:
"Be patient. Another comes. Twins."
A second later, another gush and a radiance
arrives – a fat sun after horror night. A girl,
beautiful and bawling, cow lashes, grip firm on
the tit. Dawn breaks through the window. The
hairy twin settles in its warmth, beds down on
gathered hay.
And all wonder –
"What to do? What to do?"
Plans besieged the twins as they grew. To
rupture the love between the two sisters. But
wherever they tried to hide the furry one, whatever far distant attic was her nest – her sister
would find her. Energy moves like fast water
between them. As time bangs on, the castle finds
a strange accord with the great awakener.
Her braying intelligence coughs new stories
into the midst of the court. She spills tales
of Moroccan silver and Irish gossip onto the
feasting table, and all know they are the wiser
for it.
As the second daughter's body starts to bud,
to lift towards woman, winter settles the land

121

with its great flakes of white. There is to be a feast – the first for the fair daughter to emerge, curved and available. Fresh rushes are laid, thick yellow wicks bright the dark corridors.

The father sits alone on the big seat and runs the sharpener against his loyal blade, mind cloudy with worry.

The cluck-strut and stale language of young suitors is a wearied cloak.

It's Christmas Eve.

When all are settled at table, cup lifted, honeyed chop on plate, a groan comes from outside the hall. A keening of many terrible things. From the tree line, and beyond that the lochs and mountain –

Come Witch.

Come Giant.

Come Ogre.

The gaggle-swarm churn up the frosted turf, shit on the frozen moat, hurling old, black language at the loafing warriors. Horse-leather drums thump the occult pace, skulls of snow-eagles shake atop rowan staffs. The butchers cower at table.

But the Tattered sister charges the un-killable throng.

No one blocks her path.

She is swift with the death-screech of the owl.

Fists rain-daggers, her fame a slurry of
violence, hot landed on ghoulish heads. Adrift
in this fury that has greeted them – this tiny
sister, this speck of joyous iron, a grand-general
of malice – the coven scatters, loses its mighty
shape and starts a boozy retreat.

They seem impressed.

Leaning from a window is the bright sister.
Spotted – a witch leans from a foaming mare and
twists her head clean off. From her crane-skin
bag she wrestles a calf's head onto the twitching
body but takes her face as booty, blood-mad
under the braying moon.

This mid-winter surgery has been a success.
The bewildered calf's head squats rough on the
lime-white body. The chambers ring shrill with a
mother's terror; Father grips the confirming walls.

Tatterhood is calm:

"This shape-leap
offers relief.
Rather an animal power close by,
than the violence of unready love
that was being prepared.

"As it goes, I have the sight.
I know where her head will go.

"But two lochs north

123

there is a longhouse
of Hags.

"The head will be placed on a
rusty nail.

"Me and my calf-sister
will take the foray.

"We will collect,
and with heavy penalty."

The king offers a hundred horseman, a
thousand archers, witch-killers, holy sprinklers,
coal-souled mercenaries. Beserkers.

The sisters will take none of it but a ship.
The crow caws
that this is for them alone.

One loch then the other. The nested croft of
the Blaggard Hags. The harvest is smooth as the
Goat-Sister threshes the flesh wall. The head is
scooped delicately from that nail. Placed back
on rightful shoulders with three flecks silvering
the blond.

Decision on the boat. To turn home or the
whale-road?

They settle for the vast unfurling, experience's bounty, to reach jubilation, to hang foamy
thinking like animal skins from the smoky mast.
Three, four years pass this way.

A distant port. A king in middle years, widowed – but one who leans into danger. Makes
his way through the rigging and gulls to befriend
these salty women. His son, with unsung
charisma, follows behind.

A love affair erupts between the noble and
the fair sister. A horn blows for the marriage
binding, but Tatter waves her chafed hand and
chants from the greasy hood:

"Older sisters marry first.
Root me with the son –
a double wedding."

Grief-choked, the son and father debate by
the long jetty, quietly turning life's forks in their
subtle hands. The older shape crumples at the
vastness of his son's panache.

Before long three horses and a goat take a
flowered lane to the simple chapel.

At the back Tatterhood and the son, her
goat's fur stiffened with mud, his horse
sure-hoofed, gold bridle and saddle, licked
with rubies.

"Why do men never ask the questions that
open a woman's soul?" She peers up, curious. "If
I tell you what to ask, will you ask me?"

The boy coughs and straightens.

"Certainly."

A true dowry.

"Why do I ride a goat?
Why do I carry a spoon?
Why do I wear a hood?"

"Because for one with eyes to behold it, it's not a goat!"
A Castilian steed rears up.

"Because for one with eyes to behold it, it's not a spoon!"
A rowan wand hums air.

"Because for one with eyes to behold it, it's not a hood!"
A crown of dog rose and antler bone sits aloft.

Bundled hair like dark torrent surges as a
keen sea down the small of her back. Foals
quiver on the green hill. Brandy is drunk from
the Romany's hand. We hear a pipe, a drum, the
rasp of fiddle.

Her beautiful, ordinary face gleams by the
chapel's yellow candle.

The wedding will last for years.

FURTHER READING

On the work of Victor Turner:

Turner, Victor. *The Forest of Symbols: Aspects of Ndembu Ritual*. Ithaca, NY: Cornell University Press, 1967.

On horse skulls under dance floors:

Evans, George Ewart. *The Pattern Under the Plough*. London: Faber Editions, 1966.

ABOUT THE AUTHOR

MARTIN SHAW is a mythologist, storyteller and teacher. Founder of both the Oral Tradition and Living Myth courses at Stanford University, he is also director of the Westcountry School of Myth in the UK. Dr Shaw is author of the award-winning *Mythteller* trilogy as well as *Courting the Dawn: Poems of Lorca* (with Stephan Harding), and *The Night Wages*. His conversation and essay on the artist Ai Weiwei, *Life Cycle,* was recently released by the Marciano Arts Foundation. David Abram has described Shaw's work as 'piratical brilliance'.

Alongside this, Shaw has spent twenty years as a wilderness rites of passage guide, working with returning veterans, at-risk youth and hundreds of others to establish a deep connection to nature through a four-day fast in a wild place. His book *Wolf Milk* is a reflection on this ancient practice.

Core to all his writings is a four-year period he spent living in a tent, exploring remaining pockets of English wilderness.

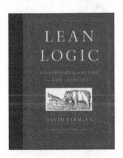

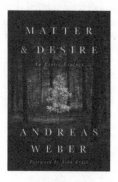